Carna

CW01467828

Severed

by

K.T. Fisher & Ava Manello

Nikki

Hope you enjoy

the continuing adventure

x

Copyright

K.T. Fisher and Ava Manello

Severed Angel

First Published 2014 by KBK Publishing

ISBN-13: 978-1499713770

ISBN-10: 1499713770

Dedication

To Emma, who has become a great friend on this crazy journey and showed us that there is light at the end of the tunnel, thank you for being our friend.

To Ellen, who made me cry with laughter when she said a scene was Foo Foo clenchingly hot.

To Diane, who may be an ocean away but is always in our hearts.

To Jane, our first fangirl. Your trailers and teasers are fantastic, your support is unbelievable, thank you for making us feel like movie stars.

To our girls, we are proud to be your mummies, but really hope you don't try reading this book until you're old enough to stop rolling your eyes at our research images on Facebook!

Love K.T Fisher and Ava Manello

xxx

Contents

Previously

Eve

Waking up slowly, I feel the heat of another body at my side. Angel looks peaceful, the stress of the last few days seems to be leaving him now. He hasn't woken with nightmares either in the last week which is a bonus. He never has told me what they're about but I leave him to it.

When Angel understood what Doc had given him I felt guilty as fuck. He was right to do it though, Angel would have been in too much pain otherwise, and he's too proud to say anything.

I look at the clock, realizing I have to make a move. It's going to break my heart to leave this man, but I need my daughter more. This isn't a life for her. It wouldn't be fair for me to bring her into the middle of this thing between Angel and I when I don't even know what's happening. My return ticket has me flying home to England in just a few hours. Angel never asked me to stay, we never discussed me going home either, but he knows I'm leaving today. He didn't say anything last night, but that's fine. I didn't really expect him to. To him this was just a casual hook up.

Whilst Teresa and I have re-built our relationship, it will never be quite the same again. I think too much happened between Elvis's death and Teresa's wedding. Certain words were spoken and can't be taken back. Other than the fact I've fallen in love with this man, there's nothing else for me here. Angel made it clear at the start he doesn't do relationships, and as amazing as the sex has been, I don't do casual. I don't like to share. I smile at the thought of seeing Elizabeth, I've missed my baby girl. There were times these past few weeks I never thought I'd get to see her again.

Rising carefully from the bed, wanting to avoid waking my sleeping hero, I head to the shower. The hot water soothes away some of the aches and pains, but I'm not sure I want them all gone. They're a memory of the smoking hot sex I've been enjoying so much of lately. Truth be told, I don't think I'll ever experience sex like that again. I want to hold on to and cherish these memories of Angel.

Pulling my hair into a loose top knot, I wipe the steam from the mirror and examine my face. Despite the hot sex of the past few days I've aged a little. There are lines and creases where there were none before, testament to the nightmare I've lived through. A permanent reminder. I dress slowly, wanting to draw out these last few moments alone with Angel, even if he is sleeping and unaware of my presence. I'll take what I can get.

There's a gentle knock at the door, signaling my time is up. Teresa stands on the other side, pulling me close when she sees the tears falling down my face. "Oh sweetie." She hugs me tight. "It's probably for the best."

She wipes a tear away, only for it to be quickly replaced by a fresh one. "You're making the right decision. You have your baby girl to think about." I know she's right, but at this moment my head and my heart are pulling me in opposite directions. Stepping away from Teresa, I move towards the bed, taking my last memory of Angel as he sleeps. I lean over, gently placing a kiss on his forehead, before turning and grabbing my bags.
As I enter the living area there's a small group of people waiting to see me off. I look over to see Sue, Diane, Dragon, Disney, Ink, Cowboy and even Prez is there. I get passed around as they hug me goodbye. Prez huffs his shoulders and gives me a quick hug, muttering "Take care."

He plants a chaste kiss on my cheek. It's obviously more emotion than he's comfortable showing as I hear him mutter "Fuck it." before quickly heading off in the direction of his office. The others take turns hugging and kissing me again.

Ink gives me an extra long hug. "I'm sorry about all that shit."

"Don't even worry about that." I hug him back, then I'm drawn into a three way hug with Diane and Teresa. There's a few tears shared.

"You better bring that beautiful girl to come and see me." Diane snuffles.

After I agree, they see me safely settled in the driver's seat of my rental car, having loaded my luggage for me. I've declined an escort. Satan's behind bars now so the threat is over. I need this last couple of hours on my own to adjust to my new reality and to maybe shed a few tears in privacy.

The journey back to the airport is uneventful. I return the hire car, moving through check in and boarding on auto pilot. The plane moves along the runway, taking off into a deep blue, cloudless sky. I can't help thinking I've made the wrong decision, but it's too late now. I'm devastated at leaving Angel but I'm so excited about seeing Elizabeth soon,

***

Gabe

I'm woken by the deep, throbbing pain in my shoulder. Fuck! Getting shot hurts.

I reach for Eve, pretty sure she can distract me with that sexy mouth of hers on my cock, just like she did last night. The sheets beside me are cold. I open my eyes to see her side of the bed empty. I don't have a good fucking feeling about this.

Struggling from the bed with only one good arm I reach for my shorts, pulling them on one handed. The clocks showing late afternoon. Doc's sneaky sedative really fucking knocked me out.

Then I see it. An envelope with my name on it is laying on Eve's pillow.

What the fuck!

I curse some more trying to get the envelope open with just my good arm and pull out a handwritten letter. Shit. Tell me this isn't what I think it is.

Gabe

I couldn't bring myself to wake you to say goodbye, you looked so peaceful sleeping. Leaving you is hard enough without having to look you in the eye as I say it. As badly as I want to stay and see where this thing between us is going, I miss my baby girl more.

I've got to be her Mummy, she needs me more right now than you do. Truth be told, I need her just as badly.

I'll never forget the short, but amazing time we've spent together, the memories of you will keep me warm when my bed is cold and lonely. And yes, the sex was fucking hot and the best I'll ever know!

Take care of yourself and thank you for keeping me safe

Eve
xxx

Fuck! Shit! Fuck!

I reach for the closest thing to me. The alarm clock and smash it against the wall, the broken pieces falling to the floor.

I can't remember what time her fucking flight was, so head out of the room in search of Teresa. She'll know, and with any luck I'll get to the airport before she leaves and fix this.

I reach the living area and don't understand what I'm seeing. Prez is cursing under his breath, Teresa is sobbing loudly and everyone looks like their dog just died. "What the fucks going on?" I question.

Prez looks up at me. Suddenly I don't want to know. The look on his face is scaring the shit out of me, Teresa's cries have gotten louder since she caught sight of me.

"Satan..." Prez stumbles with his speech. "Satan's out."

What the fuck?

How on earth is he out of jail so quickly?

"There was a fuck up on the paperwork, his bastard of a lawyer got him out on a technicality."

"Fuck, I need to get to the airport now!" I almost collapse to the floor, I'm in so much pain right now but I can't risk losing Eve.

***

The ride to the airport was hell, my shoulder felt every jar and bump in the road. Doc dosed me up on painkillers before we left. Cowboy's driven here like a bat out of hell. We're lucky he didn't get stopped for speeding the way he flew along some of those roads.

We pull up at the drop off for departures, Cowboy helping me out of the vehicle. then running back to go park. I enter the airport, where the fuck do I start looking for her.

Spotting the British Airways flight desk I pull the flight details from my pocket. Teresa had them ready for me as we set off in the truck.

The blonde assistant behind the desk looks me up and down, obviously not liking what she sees judging from the sneer on her face.

"How may I help you, sir". Fucking bitch. I hand over the flight details and she takes them slowly. Why the fuck can't she hurry up, does she not realize how important this is to me right now.

"I'm sorry sir, that flight has just departed." She gives me an odd look. "Funny that, I could have sworn I already checked you in."

I crumple to the ground in agony, I'm too late. Eve has left me. That's where Cowboy finds me.

"I'm too late" I sob into his shoulder as he tries to help me stand.
"Don't you dare give up Angel!" he chastises. "We'll sort this, I promise. That's what brothers are for." We limp back to the truck together. He's right, we'll sort this and I will get Eve back. We reach the truck, ready to head back to the clubhouse. My brothers will help me work a plan out.

I lay back against the seat, defeated for now. "I love you Eve, don't worry Princess, you're mine, and I'm coming to claim what's mine."

Previously - Epilogue

Satan

I owe my lawyer big time, the fucker came through for me. I don't know who he had to pay off, but the paperwork went to fuck and I'm back on the streets.

I grab my bag, throwing it over my shoulder as I walk into the huge building.

I see my target ahead of me, she hasn't a clue I'm here. Stupid bitch can't see anything for all the fucking tears she's wasting. This is sweet.

I keep out of her line of vision just to be sure, I don't want my surprise spoiling yet.

***

The door closes behind me, I'm the last one through. Still she can't see me, her heads bowed down, probably fucking crying again, stupid bitch.

I take my seat, scaring the shit out of the old lady at my side. I love the effect my cut has on people.

I settle back, I'm in for a long haul but this is going to be so sweet. I know my fucker of a brother set me up. Well now I'm going to pay him back, big time.

A voice comes over the tannoy "Good afternoon ladies and gentlemen. This is your captain speaking. Welcome to flight BA0016 bound for London Heathrow. We hope you enjoy your flight with us today."

I look ahead of me, Eve sit's several rows ahead, totally unaware that I'm here on the same plane as her.

I've never been to England before, I'm quite looking forward to it. But, I'm looking forward to having some one on one time with Eve even more.

To be continued...

Chapter One

Eve

The long flight home would have been a hell of a lot worse if it hadn't been for the woman sitting by my side. She'd initially taken one look at my tear stained face as I sat down beside her and left me alone. However, once we'd been in the air for a couple of hours, she decided I'd wallowed in my own misery long enough.

"I don't want to interfere honey, but are you okay?" She has such a concerned look on her face that I can't be rude and not answer her. Besides, I feel like I do need to talk to someone. The silence of holding it all in is driving me crazy, and I know my mum won't want to hear about it when I get home. I don't even think she'll notice that I'm sad.

"Not really, it's been a rough few weeks." She gives me a sad smile, and I laugh brokenly at the insanity of recent events. "I almost got killed, met the man of my dreams, and now I'm going home without him." Saying the words aloud releases a fresh bout of tears. I wipe at them and try to calm myself, but images of Gabe when I last saw him make me sad.

One hand reaches over to pat my back gently, while the other offers me a tissue which I gladly accept. I'm feeling a tiny bit better already. "Well, we've a long flight ahead of us, why don't you tell me all about it? A problem shared is a problem halved." She smiles over at me. "My name's Elle, and I'm pleased to meet you."

I turn to look at this kind stranger. She's beautiful, looks a little older than me with long blonde tresses falling past her shoulders. If it hadn't been for the ripped jeans and band t-shirt I'd have sworn she was a model. Hell maybe she is, she certainly looks the part. She also has one of those personalities that you seem to warm to, instantly. My gut tells me I can trust this woman, and this time I'm going to listen to it.

She spends the next couple of hours listening to my story after I introduce myself. Her face goes through a whole host of emotions, laughter, sadness and downright shock to horror. I guess looking back, it's the kind of thing you see in the movies or read about in books. It just wasn't supposed to happen in real life, but it did. I'm glad she doesn't seem critical of the MC way of life either. I think I would have been if our roles were reversed. Instead, she just seems concerned for me.

"Do you love Gabe?" She queries. I take a deep breath before answering her.

"When I left I thought I did, but was scared that it was just lust for him. By the time I got to the airport I knew it was true, I do love him." I hunt through my bag for my phone, it's in flight mode so I flick through some of the pictures I took during my time in Australia. I want to remember my time there. I find a picture of me and Teresa with Pres and Gabe standing behind us and show Elle. Her eyes widen as she takes in the sexy men in the picture and I nod my head. I totally understand her reaction. All that hotness in tattoos and leather is eye wideningly orgasmic.

I've just put my phone away when Elle takes my hand in hers, gently patting it. "It's not too late Eve. Go home, give your daughter the biggest and longest hug, then find a way to talk to your man and see if there's anything there on his side."

She's right, I need to talk to Gabe to find out how he really feels. If this is all one sided then I need to buck up my ideas and stop pining, and if it isn't , I need to work out what to do about it.

"Thanks Elle, I feel better for talking it through with you." Whilst I still haven't resolved my situation, at least now I have a better idea of what to do when I get home.

I realize I've been monopolizing the conversation for the last few hours and feel slightly guilty. "Enough about my troubles, why don't you tell me all about you?" I'm not just being polite, I really do want to get to know Elle better.

Elle shares that she's a freelance writer. Her current assignment is for an online travel magazine who are doing a feature on European holidays for singles. She's coming to the UK for a couple of weeks and staying in London, York, Newcastle and Edinburgh.

"I don't believe it! I live in York. Can we meet up and I'll show you the sights." I beg. It would be great to show my new friend around, and selfishly I hope it will make my return a little less lonely. Whilst I'm happy to be seeing Elizabeth again, there's only so much two year old chatter you can stand before needing adult company. For some reason I felt an instant connection with Elle.

"That would be great." Elle beams at me. Her beautiful smile lights up her whole face. "We'll sort the dates out before we land, but for now tell me more about this Ink character, he sounds yummy."

I have to laugh at her choice of words, I'm not sure yummy is a word I'd use to describe Ink. It's the sort of word you use to talk about a fit mother in the nursery playground, not a hunk of tattooed hotness in an MC club.

I tell her about his very short, dark hair, his muscled, tattooed arms, the hint of tattoos on his back and chest I'd caught glimpses of, but mostly about his character. Ink was my friend from the beginning, he was there for me when others turned their backs. Just thinking about Ink brings a smile to my face. Even though we went through an awkward stage when I found out his true feelings for me, I was glad we cleared it up before I left.

"Holy hell," Elle swoons, "you've got to set me up with an introduction when I fly home." It will be good to have an opportunity to chat to Ink again, so I assure Elle I'll do my best for her. Besides, Elle's a freaking goddess, I'm sure Ink will be grateful for the introduction.

The rest of the flight passes with mindless chatter. We find we have a lot of things in common, from favourite authors to music. By the end of the flight it feels like we've known each other forever. It's the kind of closeness I used to have with Teresa and I miss that in my life.

Satan

For fucks sake! The old biddy at the side of me is wearing me out. After looking scared of me when I first sat down, she soon seemed to overcome it and starts blathering on about her grand kids, her kids and her fucking dog. I desperately want to shut her up, perhaps I'll sort her out when we land. Until then I reach for the earphones and try to shut her out. It doesn't work but at least now it's reduced to a dull drone. Fucking annoying bitch. The in flight entertainment is lousy, Catching Fire, Paul Newman or the Hobbit! What the fuck. As if I want to watch this crap, although I 'm surprised how addictive the game Tetris is. Anything's better than listening to the old cow rattle on beside me.

The air hostess keeps giving me looks, the kind that tell me she wouldn't mind joining the mile high club if an opportunity presents itself. She'll do for a quick fuck, but she doesn't excite my dick as much as the thought of having Eve does. That bitch has been on my mind for a while now, I need to fuck her out of my system and then finally finish her.

Eve's sitting several rows ahead of me, she's finally stopped crying and seems to be chattering away with the blonde at the side of her. Now that I wouldn't mind tapping. The thought of a threesome with Eve and her new friend has me hard. Maybe I will give that air hostess a run for her money, just to relieve the tension, it will be okay as long as I don't have to look at her face.

Removing my headphones, the old biddy suddenly goes back up to full volume. Fuck me, she's never stopped prattling away at all. I give her a stern look but she's oblivious, trying to pass me photos. Enough is enough! "Look love, for the good of your health shut the fuck up and put the photos away! I couldn't give a rats shit about you or your family." I snarl. She pales, quickly pushing her photos back in her purse and pretending to show interest in the in-flight magazine. Thank fuck for that.

I need to clear my head and come up with a plan for when we land. This whole thing was last minute and I haven't been able to give it the attention and thought I'd have liked. Yes, payback has to have a plan. A fucking good one. I'm just glad my lawyer didn't fuck about any longer getting me out of jail.

I'm not stupid, if I'd been sent down I'd have been dead within days. Trust my pussy brother to come up with a dumb ass frame up instead of having the balls to deal with me himself. That's something else we don't have in common. I don't fuck around. I'll deal with this Eve bitch, then I'm going home to put an end to my brother once and for all. It used to be fun having a go at him, but it's gotten old and stale. I'm looking forward to taking him out, and I've got just the twisted, sick way of doing it, once I've shown him what's left of his most recent fuck.

He's fallen for the bitch, I could see it in his eyes that day at the compound. She's okay for a quick fuck, but other than that I don't get what he sees in her. This makes it a whole lot sweeter. It helps I've now got a mole inside the club, feeding me information, like her address. One of my brothers set it up whilst I was in holding. Even if I lose her when we land, I know where she's heading. It means I can have some fun with her before I take her out.

I lick my lips and look at the busty hostess who hasn't taken her desperate eyes from me. I stand, indicating with a head nod that I want her now. Thankfully there are toilets on my end of the plane so I won't have to walk past Eve.

I've only been in the small toilet cubicle for a couple of minutes before there's a knock. I cover my dick with a rubber, and open the door, pulling her in. Ignoring her gasp of surprise I shove her face forward against the wall. I don't want to think about who she really is. I pull up her ugly, knee length skirt, then rip off her underwear. She whimpers, "I don't know about this." She begins to beg.

"Too late now bitch. Just take my dick and shut the fuck up." I clamp my hand over her mouth, so everyone on the flight doesn't hear her, then slam into her She's not very tight, probably not her first go on a plane. Little tart. I fuck her harder, as images of Eve fill my mind. Fuck, I want to take my punishment out on her, but I'll have to make do with this girl right now. I fuck her harder and I feel wetness on my hand. She's crying, I'm not ashamed that this turns me on. It only takes a couple more thrusts and I come, fuck, that feels better. I chuck away the condom and straighten myself up. "Thanks for that." I caress her plump ass and she shivers. "For your safety, don't be telling anyone what just happened." She cries a little more and I leave her, half naked and crying.

I sit back down in my seat, happy that the old cow still doesn't say a word. That interlude was okay, but nothing compared to what I have planned for Eve. Now that I am looking forward to.

Chapter Two

Eve

The worst thing about going away is most definitely coming home again! After a long ass flight I'm now standing at the side of the luggage carousel watching what feels like half of England's luggage clunk it's way around, and still there's no sight of my bags. Elle managed to spot hers and grab them over quarter of an hour ago. She wanted to stay and wait for me though, bless her.

It's early morning, and yet the airport is buzzing with activity. The only buzz I've got going on is the headache behind my eyes. I'm so tired, but I couldn't sleep on the plane. The last month has been on constant replay in my head, stopping me from sleeping no matter how tired I am. While Elle luckily managed to catch some sleep, I kept second guessing the decisions I'd made. If I hadn't ignored Teresa's instructions I'd never have been in that store, never witnessed a gruesome murder and that means Elvis would still be alive. The guilt has been eating away at me. Then the other voice reminds me that I'd never have met Gabe. I'd never have got to experience the best sex of my life. Who am I kidding, I may have had great sex but that will always be a memory, I doubt I'll experience anything like that again, and great sex is nothing, not when the flip side is that Elvis is gone.

I'm saved from my depressing thoughts by the sight of my bag finally making its way towards me. Elle looks up from texting on her phone as she sees me move to the luggage carousel. She gives me her warm smile, before returning to her texting.

As I pull my bag towards me, I freeze and close my eyes. Quickly opening them again I relax. The lack of sleep must be catching up with me, I'm starting to hallucinate. I could have sworn I just saw Gabe over in the opposite side of the terminal watching me. I really need some sleep!

Bags in hand we head towards the tube station. Elle is going to be staying in a hotel near Kings Cross Station, and I need to head there to catch my train back to York. If we're lucky we'll make the 7:14 tube which will take us straight from the terminal to the train station.

Elle is excited about her first journey on the tube. I'm more resigned, it's almost an hour long journey, the tube's intended more for commuters than travelers. Hopefully we'll find a seat near a luggage rack but I won't hold my breath. I used to share her enthusiasm for the tube. I love people watching and on the London Underground you see all sorts of weird and wonderful people. This morning I'm too tired and too sad to enjoy the experience though.

Elle can obviously sense my mood, throwing her arm around my shoulder she pulls me in close. "I know you're sad sweetie, but just think, a few hours from now you'll be holding your baby girl in your arms." I picture Elizabeth and can feel my whole face lighting up. Elle's right, I can't wait to get home to my girl. God I've missed her so much!

As we settle into our seats on the tube, luckily managing to get next to a luggage rack, I pull up the train app on my phone. There's a train back to York at 9:30 that I'll be able to use my ticket on, meaning I'll have time to grab a coffee with Elle at the station before I leave. I could buy a new ticket for the earlier train but it's not worth the extra expense for the sake of an hour. Besides, as eager as I am to finally get home, I want just a little longer with my new found friend.

Kings Cross Station is already heaving at this time of morning. Once again I freeze before gathering myself together. Elle looks back at me, confused, I manage to give her a false smile. I'm finding myself hallucinating again, I'm sure I just spotted Gabe across the station concourse. Another traveler passes by me, blocking my line of sight, and when they're gone so is the vision. I rub my tired eyes, and try and put on a happy face for Elle who's now looking around the station in interest.

"What a beautiful station." She exclaims. They've done a lot of work here over the last few years, melding the old historic station with new modern features.

"If you think this is beautiful wait till you see St. Pancras." I tell her. They've taken the old stone buildings, added a load of glass and it looks amazing. I tell her about the champagne bar on the second level of St. Pancras, her eyes lighting up. Elle looks like the kind of woman who'd enjoy a glass or two of champagne. I'm the kind of woman who's happy with a bottle of alcopop or a vodka, I'm easily pleased and even more easily drunk.

Because of our bags we settle at a table outside a coffee shop. Elle is even more fascinated by the hustle and bustle and people watching than she was on the train. I sip on my coffee, watching the hands of the clock slowly make their way towards my departure time. There's no point in rushing, I won't be allowed through the barrier to board my train until almost the last moment.

Elle talks me through her plans for London. There are various attractions she wants to visit, and eateries she wants to sample, but in just a few days she'll be heading to York. I'm looking forward to showing her my City. I guess you get pretty jaded about the place you live, but my home town is beautiful, it attracts visitors from around the world. There's a price to that beauty though, it's an expensive place to live, although granted not as expensive as London.

Elle flicks her long blonde hair over her shoulder. You'd never guess she'd just spent hours on a flight, she looks so fresh and natural. In contrast, I look shattered and very crumpled.

We make sure we've got the correct phone numbers for each other, swap addresses and then it's time for me to bid her farewell. Don't ask me why, but this is actually quite hard. This feels like the final end to my Australian adventure, even though I know I'm going to see her again in a few days, assuming her plans don't change.

Elle hugs me tightly, whispering in my ear. "Stay strong sweetie, I'll see you soon and we'll figure out a way to get you and your hot man together again." She sounds so convincing, I almost believe her. I want to believe that she can help.

By the time I reach my reserved seat on the train I'm huffing and puffing, having had to pull my bags almost the entire length of the train to find my carriage. At least my seat reservation has worked, I fall into the seat with relief. Any flight delays and I'd have been forced to take pot luck getting a seat on a later train. The thought of having to stand all the way back to York is not a pleasant one.

The train journey takes a little over two hours. I doze lightly for most of it, managing to ignore the noise and bustle from the carriage around me. I start to spot the landmarks that signify I'm nearing home and an excited feeling stirs in my stomach. I gather my belongings together, moving to the luggage rack to reclaim my bags. For just a moment I can see straight down the aisle of the train, through to the next carriage. I see Gabe again, but just like before I blink and he's gone. This is getting really silly now. If it continues after I've had a proper sleep I'll have to make an appointment with the Doctor. I've obviously been under too much stress and it's shattered my nerves. I swear my heart skips a beat every time I think that I see him, if only.

The train draws to a halt, this platform at the far side of the station always feels so cold and gloomy, but as I look out of the window my spirits are lifted by the sight of my mother, holding a wriggling Elizabeth in her arms. My face breaks into a huge smile. She's so beautiful.

The door swoosh's open, and I step down. I'm so tired I could literally fall but nothing will stop me getting to my baby right now. Moving away from the door I drop my bags as Elizabeth comes hurtling towards me and I grab her up in my arms, squeezing tightly, afraid to let go of my precious girl.

"Hello Mummy," she grins. "Did you get me a present?" I laugh and kiss her cheek. That's my girl, more concerned about her presents than having me back. It's so good to be home.

Chapter Three

Gabe

I don't know how many times I've walked back and forth in this fucking office. It's not big enough, I need more fucking room!

I punch the wall in anger and everyone stops to look at me. When I fire a glare at them they quickly return back to whatever it is they're doing. Apart from Teresa, she's still frantically searching through a box of Eve's things that she's received over the years they've been apart. She has Eve's address written down somewhere, years of emails and talking over Skype meant there wasn't much call for hand written letters. Cowboy and Ink are supposed to be getting tickets for me to reach my girl, but they aren't fucking doing it fast enough! I growl in frustration, yanking on my hair as I begin to pace again. Prez shoots me an annoyed look. "Do you need to take a step outside, VP?"

I keep eye contact with my club president, and take a deep breath. Sitting down in the only vacant chair, I shake my head. I dig my phone out of my pocket for the hundredth time, dialing Eve's number again. Fucking voice mail! When is she going to turn her phone back on? I know she'll have it in flight mode while she's in the air but I can't help trying regardless. I lean my head back against the chair, looking up at the ceiling, taking deep, soothing breaths. I need to calm the fuck down. I need a clear head on my shoulders in order to save my girl. It's looking like it's going to take at least a day and a half to reach her, seeing as it's already been over six hours since she boarded her plane, it's too fucking long! My twisted fuck of a brother could have reached her by now and done god knows what to her. No way could I live with myself if I let him do that.

"We need that address baby." Prez crouches down in front of Teresa. His gaze softening as he looks at her. She looks a little frantic right now. When she looks up at him she has tears streaming down her face, throwing a frustrated look towards her old man.

"I'm doing my fucking best!" She starts to cry again. Prez puts his hand on her shoulder, trying to soothe her. She shrugs him off, digging through her box again. "I need to find it so we can get her back. I will find it." She's frantic.

Prez glances at me. I can tell he feels hopeless. In order to help his woman, he needs to get her best friend back. Right now, we're getting nowhere.

"I've got it!" Teresa holds a black notebook in the air. "It's right here. It's Eve's address, I have it!"

I take the book from her shaking hands, seeing Eve's name and address, neatly written on the front page. Thank fuck, that's one thing in our favor. Now we just need to book flights, then figure out how to get from the airport to Eve.

Teresa's sobs fill the room once more, she's holding onto a photo. Inside that box she has memories of their childhood, as well as photo's Eve sent her of herself and her daughter over the years. I take a step closer, hovering over her shoulder. I see she's looking down at a picture of Eve cuddling Elizabeth. Both of them are smiling widely at the camera. "What if he gets them, Bill?" She cries loudly. "Oh God, what if gets hold of baby

Elizabeth? He can't hurt them! Surely he won't hurt a baby?" I look down at the floor. I can't look at her face because I know, as well as everyone else in this room, that Satan would hurt a baby. He has no heart, no conscience. He wouldn't think twice about hurting anyone, especially a baby. "She's family Bill, they both are. He can't get to them, he can't! Please help them, please!"

Her words drift off as her sobs become louder. She crumbles on the floor, a crying, screaming heap. Prez looks over to Cowboy and Ink sitting at the laptop. "Get those flights booked now. Get over there, and bring Eve and her baby back here straight away!"

Prez leans down, lifting his old lady from the floor. She cries harder, clinging to him, pleading for her friend's life, as he carries her out of the office. I shut the door behind them, rubbing my tired eyes. I guess he won't be back for a while, he needs to take care of his woman. I decide that he's not coming with us to England. I'll take Ink and Cowboy with me. Prez needs to stay here with Teresa, no one else will be able to calm her down. She needs him right now. Ink and Cowboy will be enough back up for me. Our job is to get Eve and Elizabeth, and get them back here to safety. Then I'll persuade Eve to stay for good, I'll get to know Elizabeth. I want us to be a family. I'm going to get my woman back.

Ink walks over to me, waiting for me to look at him before he talks. I think he's pissed at me over all of this. "We've found a flight leaving in four hours. That's the earliest one we can get. Is Prez coming or is it just us three?"

"Us three, Prez needs to stay here." Ink nods, continuing to look at me. "What about once we land?"
"Have to get the train to her home city of York, we'll figure it out from there." Cowboy cuts in.

"Hopefully, she'll have turned her phone on by then, and be safe." Ink adds.

I straighten myself, stepping away from the wall. "You got something to say?"

We stare at each other until Ink takes a step back, shaking his head. "No."

I rip the page showing her address from the black book, tossing the rest of it on the floor. I spot a picture on the floor beside the discarded book and pick it up. It's the photo of Eve and Elizabeth, the one Teresa was crying over. I fold it, placing it safely in my pocket, then turning to open the office door. Before I leave, I face Cowboy and Ink. "Book those tickets for us and pack your shit." I look at Ink. "We *will* bring them back."

I slam the door behind me, marching towards my room. I can still smell Eve's scent in there. I stop in the middle of the room, breathing her in, the memory of her calming me down. As much as the way Ink acted pissed me off, he's a good guy. He'll help me get Eve back. It grated on my nerves how well they got on together, but she only sees him as a friend. Hopefully, between the both of us, we can persuade her to come back. I hope she'll understand it's the best way to ensure her and Elizabeth's safety. I just hope we get to her before Satan does.

Chapter Four

Gabe

After I've packed some basic shit to last me a couple of days, I sit on the end of my bed, gazing around my room. I can't help but see Eve everywhere I look. It's driving me fucking nuts! I pull out the photo I folded into my pocket, just staring at it, losing track of time. I look into Eve's beautiful face. I begin to stroke the image, wishing she was here so I could kiss those plump lips of hers. To know that she's safe in my arms is my biggest fucking wish right now. I pull back the anger that's sizzling just below the surface, threatening to take over me.

I am Satan's brother after all, therefore we're similar in ways that nobody else ever could be. We're bound, connected from our mother's womb, but we're so unalike in other ways. There's something different between us in the wiring that runs deep in our brains, in our veins. Our temper and fire for revenge are just some of the things we have in common. Unlike Satan though, I fight for the right reasons and the right people. Eve is mine, she's my woman and I will fight to bring her back to Australia, to the safety Severed MC can give her, and to finally bring her back to me. In my bed, in my arms and under me. I want to rightfully claim her as my old lady, mark her as mine so nobody will ever harm her again.

I look across at Elizabeth's sweet smiling face, as she clutches to her mother's side. I can't believe how much she resembles Eve. She's so beautiful. Thinking about the stories Eve told me about Elizabeth make me smile down at her picture. I'm really looking forward to meeting this little princess, and that's how I'll treat her. Just like her mum, they will both be mine to take care of, I'll treat them like the princesses they are. I want to bring Elizabeth back here, me and Eve will make a home for her, where she'll grow up surrounded by people who'll love her. Severed MC will be her family, she'll have more love and devotion than she can possibly cope with. Hopefully Eve and I will give her plenty of brothers to keep a watchful eye over her, as well as her many uncles. I smile widely as I picture her not being able to go anywhere without someone watching over her. She'll probably be pissed off as she gets older, but I want to make sure she's always safe from fuckers bothering her. She will grow up as beautiful as her mother, so I know that there'll be plenty of horny little dicks sniffing around.

I take a big deep breath to calm the tension that's filling me. Fuck I'm already feeling all protective and shit, and I haven't even met her yet! This little girl is going to be something though, my little girl. If Satan harms a hair on either of them, I will make him pay. By my own hands if I have to.

A knock on my door shakes me from my thoughts. "VP?"

It's Prez. I fold the picture carefully, placing it safely back in my pocket. When I answer the door Prez is leaning against the opposite wall, his arms folded. He looks tired, I guess Teresa's really wearing him out. "I heard you made plans and you're leaving without me."

I motion for him to step into the room, shutting the door behind us, and leaning back on it. "Think it's for the best Prez. Your old lady needs you here to look after her. So do the rest of the brothers, they need one of us. Not be any good with both the Prez and VP gone. I have Ink and Cowboy, they'll be all I need."

Prez looks relieved, nodding his head in agreement. "I agree. Good call, Angel. My woman is having a break down, I can't leave her alone right now. The women can't even get her to calm down. Being the only one she can depend on is wearing me out."

"Tickets are booked, just need to sort out what the fuck we do when we land."

"I've got in touch with our brothers down in Runaway MC. They have a chapter out in the UK that might be able to get over to Eve before you can. They'll have to vote on it in church, then ask the UK chapter to run it by their president, but hopefully they can keep a watchful eye over Eve." He takes a step closer. "I've already spread word that Satan is in England and that's he's a dangerous man. People ought to know what they're dealing with."

"Cheers Prez." I nod my head in agreement. It's not a brilliant plan, but it's the best we can do right now. We need all the fucking help we can get. It will be a few hours before we hear back though. Runaway MC will have to call church, take a vote then contact their UK chapter for them to do the same. I'm grateful for anything right now though. At least they should be able to get to Eve, just in case I'm not there in time for her.

I grab my small bag, walking out of my room with Prez following. I spot Cowboy and Ink waiting down the hall for me, I give them a nod as we walk towards them. "Ready boys? "I ask. They both give me a quick nod. Ink steps forward, patting my shoulder. "We'll get her back, VP."

"I fucking hope so brother. I really fucking hope so." I slap his back as I pass him, Prez right on my tail, Cowboy and Ink following behind. We all get into the black SUV so Prez can drive us to the airport. The only noise comes from Cowboy and Ink, they're bitching about random shit in the back, I don't have anything to say. My mind is too busy running wild, wondering if Eve is OK.

"VP?" I snap out of my thoughts. Shit, I need to stop doing that. I need my head straight if I'm going to be able to get my woman back.

"Yeah?" I look over to Prez.

He takes a deep breath. "You bring our girl back, along with her baby, VP"

I agree, just as we pull into the airport car park. We grab our small bags and step out the car. We say our goodbyes to Prez and just as I'm about to turn around and follow Cowboy and Ink, Prez stops me. "You do whatever you have to do to keep them safe."

I nod, his unspoken message received loud and clear. Satan won't be coming home if I have anything to do with it.

I walk into the airport, eager to board the plane that will take me to Eve and Elizabeth.

***

I walk off the last step, my feet finally hitting concrete. I quickly zip up my leather jacket, fucking hell it's cold over here. I motion for Cowboy and Ink to follow me. I'm so fucking glad to be off that plane! Don't get me wrong, everyone did their best to ignore us, but fucking hell there are some annoying people out there!
I turn my phone back on, it begins to sound a text alert straight away. It's from Prez.

PREZ: Runaway UK charter agreed. On their way to the address my old lady found.

Finally, some good news. That was sent two hours ago. At least my woman won't be alone. Hopefully they got there before Satan. Another text from Prez, sent straight after the first, shows directions that the Runaway UK charter provided. Well that's lucky, seeing as we're in a foreign country and I don't know where the fuck I'm going.

We make our way out of the airport, heading for the tube as per the directions. I try and ring Eve again, but still no fucking answer.

Just being in the same country as Eve is finally helping to control my nerves.

I'm coming baby. Just hold on a little longer.

Chapter Five

Elle

I step out of the hotel door into the crisp London air. Glancing at my watch I realize Eve should have made it home by now. I smile at the mental image of her reuniting with her daughter. That woman adores her daughter you can tell. I pull my iPhone from the back pocket of my skinny jeans and see I haven't had a text message from her yet. I'm sure she'll send one when she's settled back at home, she's probably too busy fussing over her daughter and hopefully trying to get back to that hottie of hers. There's a nagging feeling in my gut though, telling me Eve needs me, but I brush it aside as I head off for the nearest tube station to begin my adventure. Probably nothing, just me worrying uselessly.

London is everything I hoped it would be. It's multicultural, a fascinating mix of heritage and modern, and it's busy and bustling. I don't think I could live here. I prefer a quieter, smaller city, but I plan on making the most of the tourist attractions for the few days I'm here.

With my bus ticket in hand I head towards the red double decker tour bus. I've been told it's the best way to take in London, then tomorrow I can jump on and off the bus to visit the sights as I wish. Over the next few hours I take in the potted history of London, the Houses of Parliament are a bit dreary looking but when we get to Buckingham Palace, wow! I definitely want a closer look at that and The Tower of London.

My ticket also gives me access to a river tour down the Thames. The Captain acts like an un-official tour guide, he's hilarious. I jump off at Greenwich and wander round the beautiful old buildings, before grabbing a coffee and heading back for the return boat.

Throughout the day I can't shake the feeling that something is wrong. I can't put my finger on it. I quickly discard the notion that it's jet lag, I travel too much for that to affect me like this. Checking my phone I see I still haven't heard from Eve, and the gnawing sense that something is wrong eats at me.

I'm not a psychic, but I have learned to trust my sixth sense on occasion. Right now it's telling me Eve needs me. I know I've only just met her, but our connection feels deeper than that. I know we will be great friends. I decide that I'm heading to York tomorrow, it's earlier than I'd planned to, but I can adjust and fit London in at the end of my trip instead.

Decision made I already feel better. I head back to my hotel, I'll eat in the restaurant there tonight and catch an early train out of Kings Cross in the morning.

***

Eve

I'd forgotten just how good it felt to hold my baby girl in my arms so I squeeze her a little bit harder. God, I've missed her. There were times in Australia when I'd see something she would love so I'd turn to show it to her. then feel stupid because she wasn't there. It's typical of my girl to ask for her presents before she even gives me a kiss. Laughing I pass her the carrier bag in my hand. Most of her gifts are safely stored in my luggage, but this one is perfect to give her now.

Elizabeth excitedly digs into the bag then pauses, a look of concentration on her face as she reaches in and takes out her gift. Her eyes light up as she pulls the cuddly Koala free of its wrapping, then squishes it close to her chest. "That's a present from our friend Gabe, baby." She looks up, uncertainty visible in her expression. "You remember Gabe don't you, from when you spoke to Mummy on Skype?"

I can't believe she's forgotten him already. I almost laugh at her cute little expression while she thinks about it. Her face suddenly lights up in remembrance. "You mean my Angel? Silly mummy," she laughs while shaking her head at me, cuddling the Koala closer. "Angel is my special fwiend, he says I'm pwetty."

My heart warms up, remembering that particular Skype call. I'd been cuddled up against Gabe's chest as he chatted away with my girl. She'd been so enchanted to have a new friend she'd practically forgotten I was on the call too. After that, whenever I spoke to her, she would ask where her Angel was.

"Where's Angel gone, mummy?" Elizabeth queries."He's disappeared." She looks round the near empty station platform, a puzzled look on her face, as though she honestly expects to see him.

I bend at the knees so I'm almost eye level with her, smoothing her hair behind her ears. "He's back in Australia, baby. He lives there like Auntie Teresa." I plant a soft kiss on her forehead, getting up to give my mother a hug. She's patiently waited in the background allowing me time to fuss my daughter. She surprises me by giving me a peck on the cheek and welcoming me home.

"No mummy." Elizabeth smiles and shakes her head. "You silly. Angel's here, I sawed him. Over there." She points to the end of the platform, frowning when she doesn't see him there. Bless her, Elizabeth has a habit of seeing things she wants when they're not there. Perhaps that's what's wrong with me, I so desperately want Gabe to be here that I'm imagining him everywhere.

"Hush now Lizzy, let's get your Mummy home. Poor thing looks shattered. I'm sure she'd like nothing more than to curl up on the sofa with you and cuddle. What do you say?" I flash my mother a grateful smile, together the three of us head out of the station to the taxi rank. As I hold Elizabeth's hand all the way I feel her lagging as she looks around, probably trying to see if she can still find Gabe.

I'm home and it's time to settle down to my old life. I need to forget all about Australia. I grab my phone from my bag, meaning to send a couple of texts to let people know I've arrived home safely, groaning when I see the black screen. It's dead. One day I'll remember to buy a portable charger. No worries, I'll charge it up when I get home, if I can remember what bag I packed the charger in.

***

Satan

I stand in the corner of the station, hidden in the shadows. I'm watching Eve's touching reunion with her family. That damned kid of hers nearly ruined everything.
Looking back I can't remember ever seeing a look of love like that on my mother's face. Come to think of it, I can't recall ever seeing a look of love on any woman's face when they looked at me. Sure, I've fucked plenty, but that's lust, not love. I shake off the sentimental shit, watching as Eve leaves the station.

My cock is hard as I think of what I'm going to do to Eve when I get her alone. I'll make sure Angel hears every scream one way or the other, and I'll make sure she's begging for him with her last breath. I shrug my bag back over my shoulder, following the happy family to the taxi rank. Soon... It's going to happen soon and I can't fucking wait.

Chapter Six

Satan

Fuck! I stare at my phone screen, the message taunting me. I don't know how he managed it so quickly, but my informant tells me Angel is on his way to York already. That means I'll have to change my plans because the timescales been reduced. Angel could arrive any fucking minute. Instead of playing with Eve like I had planned to, I'll have to kill her quickly. Fuck! I hate it when my fun's cut short. I wanted to capture her, torture that pretty little body of hers and make her scream so loud her throat hurts as she shouts Angel's name when she breathes her last breath.

The bitch hasn't even left the house yet, I'm guessing she's crashed out sleeping. I've been watching the house since she got back yesterday afternoon. I'm tired as fuck, but I can sleep when this is all finally over. The adrenalin of planning a kill as good as this will keep me going for the next few hours at least. The old cow is still in the house with her or I'd have already broken in. The way these houses are connected to each other I can't afford for anyone to raise the alarm. I need to get Eve when she comes out on her own.

I hide in the shadows, my favourite place, and watch as the bedroom window curtains are pulled open. Eve looks out directly at my hiding place, it's as though she can sense I am here. I see her shake her head then she moves out of sight. I settle in, she'll come out at some point this morning I'm sure, and when she does, I'll be waiting for her.

***

Gabe

What a fucking hellish way to travel. I miss my bike, the open air and wide spaces. The tube from the airport to the train station was awful, it's a fucking tin can underground that flashes along at speed, but it's full of noise and chatter and weird people. Ink and Cowboy were laughing at my obvious discomfort, the fuckers. It didn't help that this big, fat, ugly mama sat right next to me, practically on top of me due to her size, and wouldn't shut the fuck up the entire time. She seemed oblivious to the fact I was ignoring her, prattling on about everything and nothing as I tried to tune her out. Cowboy started making childish gestures at the two of us as him and Ink laughed, that fucker will get his when we get off this bloody contraption.

Thankfully the tube finally arrives at our station, good job Cowboy was watching the signs, I haven't got a clue what the fuck we're doing or where the fuck we're going. I also haven't got a phone signal this far underground and I'm going crazy not being able to get in touch with Eve.

The walk from the tube platform to the station feels like it goes on forever. How many bloody escalators do we have to go up for fucks sake! When we arrive above ground we're on the station concourse, I take in a deep breath of fresh air. That's better. It's still cold on the station, this whole bloody country is cold to me. I just want to grab Eve, go get Elizabeth and get the fuck back home.

I turn as I hear Ink let out a loud wolf whistle. I see his attention is on a stunning blonde who's looking at the departure board. He was too loud as half the travelers in the station turn to look at him in annoyance. Except for the blonde, she turns to look and stares. She looks between Ink and me, to Cowboy and then back to me and finally to Ink. Her face turns white, her hand coming up to her mouth. She looks shocked to see us and the next thing I know she's running towards us, what the fuck?

"It can't be. Oh my god, is it really you?" The blonde looks from me to Ink, recognition written all over her face, but I've no idea who the fuck she is.

"Excuse me?" I ask, my words are almost unheard as Ink moves in.

"Well hello beautiful, do we know each other? I think I would have remembered you." He's oozing that fucking charm of his. Wide smile, flexing his muscles. I want to slap him, we're not here to pick up pussy for him. We're here for Eve. We don't have time for this crap.

I'm just about to put him straight when the blonde speaks. "No, you don't know me but I'm pretty sure you're Angel, Ink and Cowboy right?" She cocks an eyebrow at us in question.

"Who the fuck are you and how do you know who we are?" I growl. The only people who know we're here are our club and Runaway MC and I'm pretty certain they wouldn't have sent a fucking chick to meet us at the station. There were no plans to meet us at all.

"I'm Elle," Blondie holds her hand out in greeting. I'm still too shocked to acknowledge it, but Ink pulls it to his mouth and kisses it. The girl unsuccessfully tries to hide her smile and she looks back to me. "I met Eve on the plane and she told me all about you guys." She looks at me and blushes. Fuck, what's Eve been telling her? Then it registers, this chick knows Eve, she's seen her.

"You what?" Ink stumbles over the words. "This is fucking unbelievable."

"Eve and I sat next to each other on the plane. She didn't look so good, kept crying. She told me what happened, don't worry I'm not going to say anything. She showed me her photos from her trip and I recognize you from them." She pauses as she looks over at Ink, there's something in her eyes. Shit, I think she fucking fancies him! "Anyway, we just sort of clicked and we arranged to meet up in a few days when I finished visiting London. I just got this awful feeling that something was wrong so I'm heading there today instead." She looks over at me expectantly.

"Have you spoken to her since she got back?" I still can't get past her voicemail when I call. Elle shakes her head.

"I keep trying. She was going to text me when she got back yesterday lunchtime, but nothings come through and all I get is her voicemail when I try her."

I groan. Eve has a habit of forgetting to charge her phone, at least I hope that's all that's wrong. "Well pretty lady, we're heading to see Eve ourselves, why don't you join us?" Ink offers Elle his arm, and blow me she fucking takes it.

"I'd love to." She smiles widely at him. She goes a little quiet and looks across to me. "Can I ask, is Eve in danger? I just have this feeling something's wrong." Elle looks worried, she bites on her lower lip and I see that it's having an effect on Ink. His dark eyes zero in on her mouth.
I shake my head. "It's a long story, but yes, she's in danger. So the sooner we get on this fucking train the better." I storm off to the platform indicated on the departures board, not worrying about whether the rest of them are following.

***

Elle

Holy hotness. Ink looked good in his photos but they sure didn't do the real him justice. He's a walking sex advertisement. That said, the other two guys aren't too shabby looking either. Okay they're fit as hell too, but looking at them doesn't make my heart flip the same way it does when I look at Ink. He's a player, that much is obvious. The way his eyes sweep over me and his well practiced words, but I can't resist the obvious lust in his deep brown eyes when he checks me over.

I'm still shocked over bumping into the guys at Kings Cross, but I guess I've always believed in Fate. The guys managed to get us all seats together with a table on the train, and over the past hour they've been filling me in on the scary new developments. At least they're being honest with me about just how much risk Eve is in from Satan.

I startle as my phone alerts me to an incoming text message. I'm so eager to hear from her that I almost drop my phone in excitement. When I see it's from Eve I feel so relieved. I must have gasped out loud as the guys are watching me with sudden interest. "It's a text from Eve!" I quickly swipe my finger across the phone to read her full message. She's home, she's safe and she's sorry her phone died on her yesterday. She hopes I'm having fun in London and not misbehaving too much. See, I knew this girl got me. I unconsciously smile, but the next line causes my smile to drop. Angel almost tears the phone from my hand when he sees the expression on my face. Eve writes that she thinks she's losing her mind, she's convinced she sees Angel around every corner, and now her daughter has started saying the same. Realizing the importance of those last two lines I pass the phone to Angel. I'm temporarily struck dumb, and he needs to know what's happening. He curses loudly as he reads through the message then passes the phone to Cowboy and Ink. They frown down at the phone, cursing without care.

"How do I reply?" I finally find my words. "Do I tell her about Satan. That you guys are here, or what?"

Angel pauses. Deep in thought for a moment, he's mulling over the options. "Don't tell her about Satan or me being here." He looks to the other guys as if seeking confirmation and they both nod their agreement. "Tell her you've changed your plans and are on your way to York to see her, see if she'll agree to meet you at the Station."

I nod my agreement then think of Elizabeth. "What about Elizabeth, shall I ask Eve to bring her?" Angel's brow creases further when I mention the little girl.

"No, don't mention Elizabeth for now. I'm sure Eve said she had playgroup or something most mornings anyway. She needs her daughter safe, just in case Satan is following her. I don't want any harm to come to our girl." The strain is starting to show on Angel's face. His blue eyes have lost a little of their sparkle in the time since we received the text message. I didn't miss how he called Elizabeth our girl, that warms me a little. Angel turns to Cowboy. "Get onto Prez and find out what's happening with that Runaway charter. They should have had eyes on her by now." Cowboy starts typing away on his phone, while Ink and Angel confer quietly on the best way for me to reply to Eve. It's settled, we go with the planned message we already suggested. I send Eve a friendly text letting her know I changed my plans, asking if there's any chance she can meet me when the train gets in shortly.

Time stands still waiting for her reply

Eve: I'll be there when your train gets in, can't wait to see you again!

A little of the tension leaves the atmosphere around the table when we receive her text, in a little over an hour we'll be arriving in York, and I for one feel better knowing Angel and the guys are here to help protect Eve.

***

Eve

I'm feeling giddy knowing my new friend will be here soon. I'm really looking forward to seeing her again. I wonder why she decided to change her plans? I'm sure there'll be a man involved from what little I know of Elle already.

I hear my mother shout that she's taking Elizabeth to nursery so I run down to give her a hug and a kiss before she leaves. I wanted to take her but my mother's got into a routine now, and she's going straight to the Doctors after dropping her off, which is next door to the nursery. Even though I'm still tired from all the traveling, the selfish part of me wanted to keep Elizabeth home with me today. I've missed her so much, but she's excited about seeing her friends and doesn't seem to have missed me as much as I missed her. That's kids for you I guess.

After plastering my girl with kisses, and hugging her to the point I almost crush her I let her go. I'm already dressed so grab my bag, deciding I'm going to walk part of the way with them anyway. I'll just catch the bus from the stop near the nursery. I walk down the street holding my girls hand, as she chatters away in her baby talk. She's telling me all about her little friends and what she's going to do today. As we near the bus stop I see the bus coming round the corner, I quickly kiss Elizabeth goodbye, shout bye to my mother and run for the bus. I make it just in time, gasping out my destination and handing over my change. Shit, I need to start going to the gym or something, I'm so unfit!

A hooded figure is running towards the bus but is out of luck. The doors close behind me and the bus pulls away leaving the poor traveler stranded and waiting for the next bus. Who knows, with this village it could be ten minutes or forty. I slide into a vacant seat and scroll through the books in my Kindle app. I'll arrive in plenty of time before Elle's train so I'll catch up on some reading in the meantime.

***

Satan

For fucks sake! Is the fucking driver blind? I was standing outside the door when he shut it in my fucking face. He's lucky I didn't see his face so I can't pay him a little visit. Eve caught me by surprise when she suddenly changed direction and sprinted for the bus. At least I know where she's headed, I heard her mention the station just before the door shut in my face.

I'm just about to hit something when fuck me, another bus pulls up. The driver looks at me in disgust when I don't have the correct change for the fare. I just gave him one of these stupid paper notes. He huffs a little as he hands my change over in small coins. Fucker.

As the journey progresses I can glimpse Eve's bus in front of us. Fuck, the traffic is slow here. We're forever stopping at lights, and even when they change to allow traffic to move we're stuck at a standstill. Eve's bus is making slightly better progress than ours, but not much.

I look at my phone, there are no updates from my contact. Eve hasn't got any luggage with her, so I've no idea why she's heading for the station. I hope it's not to meet that fucking twin of mine. He's already making me speed my plans along, if he's here then shit, I've got to think fast. I hate being out of my comfort zone, I've got no access to resources here, I don't even have a bike, I'm stuck on this fucking crawling bus with people I don't want to be fucking near. I'm pretty sure I could have covered the distance faster if I'd walked!

Eve's bus pulls up at a stop round the corner from the station and I'm surprised to see her jump off. I head to the front of the bus, the driver catching my eye, "This is your stop for the station mate, this is as close as we get on this route. Just walk round the corner there and you'll see it."

I get off the bus where the driver suggests, looking around for Eve. I eventually catch sight of the back of her just passing through the huge stone archway, heading in the direction of the station. I pick up my pace, being careful not to get too close to her. There aren't enough people to lose myself in around here at the moment. I'm enjoying freaking her out every now and then, giving her odd glimpses of me, but only when I know I can duck out of sight quickly. Stupid bitch probably thinks she's seeing Angel, think again Eve, I'm even better and I will show you just how much better I am soon.

Eve walks straight through the station entrance, pausing in front of the departures board. Fuck, I hope she's not going somewhere. She obviously doesn't see what she wants so she moves over to the information desk. I manage to sneak close enough to hear her. "Excuse me, can you tell me what platform the London train is due in on?"

"Which London train love? We've got them arriving every twenty minutes or so."

"I don't know, I forgot to ask her. I just know she's arriving at 11:27." Eve looks at her phone, frustrated. "I'll see if I can find out."

The assistant looks at her with understanding. "You could always just wait at the bottom of the staircase, they'll either come in on platform one which is next to you, or platform ten and you'll see them coming over the bridge."

I watch as Eve thanks her, then walks over to the coffee stand at the side of platform one. I look at my watch, we've got about 45 minutes before the train is due in. I ease back into the shadows, hoping to use the time to put a plan together.

***

Eve

I've no signal on the station so I can't text Elle to get a better idea of which train she's on. I decide to grab a coffee, and sit outside the cafe so I can do a bit of reading while I wait. From here I can see both platform one and the stairs leading to the bridge for the far platforms.

I'm engrossed in my book when I half hear an announcement. I check the time on my phone and realize Elle should be here any minute. I down the last of my coffee, tuck my phone in my pocket and move out of the cafe area. A trickle of people starts coming over the bridge so a train must have arrived at the far platform. I look up at the same time as I hear Elle calling my name and see her just stepping onto the bridge, looking stunning as ever. My jaw drops though when I see who she's with! Three men I have come to love over the past month are stood right behind her. How and why are they here?

I clasp my hand over my mouth as I gasp in shock. I'm delighted to see them and suddenly I need to be over there. I need to be with them! I can't wait for them to get over the bridge.

There's a whooshing sound as a train starts pulling off the platform near me. I see Elle's face change, she looks terrified. I hear her scream as I feel myself start to fall, I feel as if I am floating. My feet are off the ground as someone shoves into me roughly. I think I hear myself scream as I start to fall off the platform, grasping at air. The noise of the approaching train is the last thing I hear.

Gabe

It feels like it takes forever to get off this shitty train. The aisles were full of people queuing to get off at least ten minutes before we even approached the station. They're not exactly in any rush as they slowly gather their belongings from the overhead racks, blocking the narrow aisles with their fat asses which pisses me off. For fucks sake, I need to get moving, Eve's out there waiting. Elle puts her hand on my arm, trying to calm me down. The stress is obviously evident on my face. She's just beaming, she's so excited to be seeing Eve again. Even though we've told her about Satan she's not really grasped how dangerous he is. A quick look at my brothers tells me they're anxious.

Finally we start heading up the staircase, it leads to a bridge running over the tracks. Elle suddenly shouts out Eve's name, waving to the far side of the station. I turn and see her, my beautiful woman. I can see when Eve notices me as her hand goes to her mouth then she turns to come meet us. She looks excited and I need her in my arms right now.

At the same time I spot a hooded figure run up behind her. Elle screams out a warning but Eve's oblivious. I watch in horror as the figure apparently stumbles into Eve as she's heading for the stairs, it's just enough momentum to knock her from the platform. I look on in horror as I realize it's the same line a train is pulling out on. I hear Ink and Cowboy shout and we start to run. The hooded figure pauses for a second, looking right up at me and smirking. Fuck, that's when I realize it's my brother, Satan. Before I can reach him, he's vanished from sight behind the oncoming train as it struggles to brake to avoid Eve who lays broken on the track in front of it.

Chapter Seven

Gabe

There's a hellish screech as the train driver hits the brakes and don't ask me how, but he manages to pull the train to a stop, literally a hairs breath away from where Eve is laying broken on the track. It only took seconds for the whole scene to play out, but I'd swear that moment lasted an eternity. My heart is almost breaking out of my chest as I race over the distance on the bridge, desperate to get down there to my woman.

I'm oblivious to the activity around me, until I'm brought up short just as I'm about to jump down to the track. I turn, a deathly threat visible on my face, to find a policeman grasping my arm.

"Fucking let me go, that's my woman down there!" I yell. His hand falters for just a moment. In that second, his grip loosens, and without waiting for permission I'm out of there. I drop down to the track and rush over to Eve, dropping to my knees at her side. I hold back my scream of pain as I look down at her, oh god baby.

I'm vaguely aware of Ink and Cowboy talking to the policeman I just left behind, but right now I just don't care. All I care about is Eve, who lays unconscious. There's another policeman at Eve's side, gently checking her over, talking into his radio at the same time.

I grasp Eve's hand, the only part of her I dare touch. It still feels warm, there's still a chance I haven't lost her

"Sir, sir?" I become aware of the policeman trying to talk to me. "I take it you know this lady?"

"She's my woman." I growl in response.

"I need you to stay calm, there's an ambulance on its way and an emergency bike paramedic should be here any time. She's alive, I don't want to move her in case we cause any problems, so I need you to stay calm for me, and just keep talking to her."

I glance over at Eve's face. I can barely see it for the blood all over it. Her hair is half covering her face. I gently draw her hair back. I can see a faint pulse in her neck. I'm checking her over with my eyes as best I can, aside from the visible damage from the fall and landing on the gravel, she looks okay. No obvious breaks, but a nasty bump on the side of her head. "I'm here for you princess, I've got you now, I'll keep you safe." I whisper in her ear, planting the gentlest of kisses on her forehead.

What the fuck is taking the ambulance and the medic so long? No longer have I thought it than a paramedic in biker gear jumps down onto the track next to us. He quickly examines Eve, and tells us the ambulance will be here any moment. Meanwhile the police officer helps him place Eve on a backboard, just to be safe. They're securing her to the board and covering her with a blanket when the ambulance drives straight onto the platform.

***

I've no idea how long the ambulance ride to the hospital took. I just sat in the back numbly holding Eve's hand, praying for her to open those beautiful blue eyes of hers. The ambulance technician was talking the whole time, giving the driver status updates, telling me what he was doing, and yet I didn't hear a word of it. My entire being was focused on Eve. That's until we hit the ER doors.

A nurse kept dragging me away from Eve and I almost lost it till the fat security guard gave me a warning. They wouldn't let me go with her, so I had to go through to the waiting room and check her in. Fuck! This is the woman I love and I struggled to answer their questions. I couldn't tell them her phone number, just her address. I couldn't tell them her date of birth even, just the date of her birthday. I could have told them the color of her eyes is blue, I could tell them she has the cutest little raspberry birthmark just below her tattoo. I could tell them how it feels to draw my hand across her soft skin, or how I am the luckiest guy on earth when she looks straight into my eyes and tells me she's mine. But I can't answer these basic bloody questions. I feel like I know Eve, but apparently not everything.

There's a ruckus at the doorway and Ink, Cowboy and Elle come rushing in. Shit, I'd forgotten all about them.

"Where is she?" Elle cries.

"They won't let me in." I hang my head. "We've got to answer these questions for them, so they can get her checked in." Elle comes to stand beside me, wrapping her arm around me and faces the receptionist.

"Okay, what do you need to know?" She surprises me by knowing most of the answers they need, and where she doesn't she's given them contact information for Eve's mother. The police will go and get her.

We're directed to sit in the waiting area, and we wait, and we wait, and we fucking wait some more. Eve's mother rushes in at some point on the arm of a policeman, but before I can realize who she is, she's gone. They've taken her through the ER doors that they won't let me pass through.

It's another three hours before I see Eve's mother again.

***

Eve

I'm aware of pain throughout my body. Fuck, it feels like I've been hit by a truck. I don't want to open my eyes but someone is calling my name. I turn to the sound and crack my eyes open to see my mother standing at the side of me. Her face is tear stained and she looks like hell.

"Eve, please wake up for me. I'm so sorry, please wake up." I can't remember ever hearing that tone in my mother's voice before. I'd swear that's affection I can hear. I fight to open my eyes a little more and she notices. "Thank god! Oh baby, I'm so glad you're awake. I've been so worried about you."

"What happened?" I whisper.

"You had an accident. The Doctors are checking you over now." No shit Sherlock. I'd guessed that it was an accident from the pain I'm in, but she doesn't seem too keen to tell me what happened. I struggle to find a memory to let me know what caused this. The last thing I remember is holding Elizabeth's hand as we walked to nursery.

"Elizabeth!" I scream and my mother rushes over.

"She's safe, she's okay, she wasn't with you. Sharon fetched her from nursery and took her back to hers for now."

Relief floods through my body, but I still don't know how I ended up here. My head is fuzzy and I can't focus properly. The curtain opens and a young doctor walks into the room. She doesn't look any older than me, early twenties maybe. She's smartly dressed under her open white coat. "Now then Eve, I hear you've been through the wars. Let's have a look at you." She flashes a light in my eyes, asks me what feels like a million questions, prods and pokes me all over and finally stands back looking serious.

"We're a little concerned about the blood loss Eve; can you tell me when your last period was?" I try and think back. I honestly can't remember. I know I didn't have one in Australia. What's she asking me this for? I shake my head as my answer. "Is there any chance you could be pregnant?" I almost laugh at her question. I can't remember the last time douche bag touched me, and I'm on the pill anyway.

"I'm on the pill, I can't be pregnant." I answer confidently.

"Have you had unprotected sex at all?" The doctor asks the question so clinically it makes sex sound like a dirty act.

"Well, yes. Over the last three or four weeks I have, but I'm on the pill." I whisper. It's not possible. I can't be pregnant with Gabe's baby.

The doctor looks at me in sympathy, I'm not sure why. "Eve, we think you might have been pregnant. An early pregnancy, and that your body is aborting the fetus."

I want to laugh at her, to tell her how stupid that sounds, but there's a part of me that hears the word pregnant and rejoices. Then I hear the rest of her words and am hit by grief. I might have been pregnant but I'm not now.

The doctor sends me off for a scan. It's a humiliating and scary experience. Because they believe it was an early pregnancy they have to do an internal scan which looks like a bloody vibrator, covered in a condom. The technician looks at the screen, and coldly and clinically informs me that there was a pregnancy, but that it is no longer viable. How can she use language like that, that's my fucking baby she's talking about, not a lab experiment! I'm wheeled back to the ER, tears streaming down my face, and my mother trying to console me. There's nothing she can say that will make this any better, and I turn on her.

"Tell me what the fuck happened! What did I do, why have I lost my baby?" I scream the words at her. I know it's not her fault, but that doesn't change what's happened.

"The policeman told me the witnesses said someone stumbled against you at the station, and you were too close to the edge of the track sweetie. You fell back and landed on the track, it was quite a drop." I hear her voice quiver a bit at the end.

"What was I doing at the station?" Then I remember. I remember going to meet Elle, being excited to see her again, and then I remember seeing her on the bridge and Gabe was with her.

"Where's Gabe? I need Gabe." I sob. My mother looks at me confused. She has no idea who Gabe is. "My friends were at the station, that's who I was supposed to be meeting. Please go find them for me, they must be frantic. Please mum, I need Gabe." My mother looks unsure, I can tell she doesn't want to leave me yet, no matter how much I beg and plead.

Just when I think she's about to cave, the doctor comes back into the cubicle. "Right Eve, I've got the results here. I'm sorry but it looks like you were in the very early stages of pregnancy, the fall caused some damage to the placenta. It's too late to save the baby I'm afraid. What it means is that we need to take you up to theatre, we need to perform a D&C to make sure we remove all traces of the placenta so you don't get an infection." She carries on explaining the procedure to me, the reason for it, but all I can hear is that they are scraping my baby away from inside of me. I can't believe this is happening to me.

"An orderly will be along to take you up to the gyno ward and they'll take care of you from now on. There's a slight risk of concussion so we'd like to keep you in overnight after the procedure, just to keep an eye on you." She pats my hand and leaves the cubicle.

My mother is sobbing at my side. She looks at the grief on my face and comes over to pull me into a hug. "I'll get you settled on the ward then I'll go see if I can find your friends." She offers. I don't say anything in return, I can't think of what to say. The doctor's words have left me mute.

Friends... Is that all Gabe is to me? A friend? Why is he here anyway, did he decide he did have feelings for me after all? In fact why are Ink and Cowboy here as well? Something's not right about this whole situation. How the hell do I tell Gabe I was pregnant, and that I lost it because of a stupid fall, a silly accident? How can life be so cruel as to give me a gift like that and then take it away in a second?

The orderly appears. He's a cheerful guy who chatters away to my mother as he wheels me along the bland white corridors and into a lift. He's telling me they'll soon get me comfortable on the ward and take care of me. Yeah, how will I ever be comfortable again knowing I killed Gabe's baby with an act of stupidity.

***

Gabe

I've sat. I've stood. I've walked. I've paced. I've even been outside and hit my fist against a brick wall, but there's been no news of Eve. Then her mother appears. She looks like she's an old woman, although I know she's only middle aged. Her face is tear stained and she looks grief stricken. She approaches the reception desk and has a short conversation with them, and then the receptionist points her over in our direction.

I stand. Fuck, please don't let it be bad news.

"Are you Gabe?" She asks. She doesn't look me up and down and scrutinize me as I'd have expected. Her voice is so weary I doubt she's got the energy left. She just looks at me.

"Yes, I'm Gabe. You're Eve's mother? How is she?"
"I think we'd better go sit down, seems I have a lot to tell you." She gestures to the hard plastic chairs where we were just sitting.

Eve's mother spends the next few minutes reassuring us that Eve will be fine, but then the bottom drops out of my world with her next words. She tells us that Eve hadn't realized she was pregnant. It happened while she was in Australia, and sadly the accident caused her to lose the baby.

"Eve was pregnant?" Elle gasps. At least she could find the words; I'm fucking lost for them. I sat there numb. If Eve was pregnant it must have been mine. I know she wasn't with anyone else whilst she was out in Australia. We made a baby, half me and half her. And now it's gone, just like that.

"Accident?" Cowboy questions, a puzzled look on his face.

"The policeman told me there was an accident at the station. Someone stumbled into Eve and she fell onto the track." Holy fuck! They don't know that this was deliberate? "My daughter seems quite desperate to see you all, but you're going to have to wait until she's out of surgery, so while we wait why don't you fill me in on just what's been happening. How come you three are here the day after she gets home?" Eve's mother is obviously a smart lady. Her eyes linger on me.

As much as I want to see Eve and hold her right now, I know they won't let us in for hours yet, so taking in a deep breath I sit back and tell Eve's mother everything that happened while her daughter was in Australia.

***

Eve

I hate coming round from anesthetic. I feel dopey, my mouth is dry and it feels like something died in there. I'm guessing I'm due some pain killers as I hurt everywhere, but nowhere more than my stomach.

I place my hand below my stomach, remembering where Elizabeth's tiny baby bump used to sit, and I whisper sorry to my lost child. Sorry seems so inadequate really.

The door cracks open and I see Gabe peering into the room. My heart lifts for a moment at the sight of him. God, I need my man right now. The thought and elation are fleeting though, as guilt is a much stronger emotion, and it smacks me right in the face as he enters the room, smiling.

"Princess. Thank fuck you're okay. I've been going crazy out here waiting for you to wake up." He moves to the side of the bed, leaning down to place one of his gentle kisses on my forehead. I need him to grab me and hold me tight, not be gentle with me. I'm guessing he's not going to want to know me in a few minutes when I tell him what I have to say.

"Gabe, sit down a minute, there's something I've got to tell you." I look down at my hands; my fingers are twisting and knotting together. Gabe spots this, gently prizing my hands apart and holding them in his own.

"Princess, it's okay. I know, your mom told me. I'm sorry I let you go, this is all my fault." I can see grief in his face, but I'm not sure if it's for the baby, or guilt.

"How is this your fault? I'm the one who fell off the fucking platform." I hiss. I'm angry, I know I shouldn't be angry at Gabe, but right now he's the one that's here and the one I need to vent on.

"Fell? Princess, it was fucking Satan that pushed you off! He's been following you." I see a look of guilt on his face. I don't understand, I must still be drowsy or something because I'm sure he just said Satan pushed me off. That couldn't be true.

"But Satan's in jail. This is all over." I whimper.

"No princess, the police fucked up somehow. His lawyer got the charges dropped and he was on the same plane here as you. I've been scared out of my fucking wits for the past few days trying to get here and keep you safe. Speaking of which woman, you need to make a habit of making sure you have your phone on. When I do get here, I had to stand there and fucking watch while that psycho pushed you in front of a fucking train!" There's a hard edge to his voice now. Restrained anger tensing up his body.

"But the police told my mother it was an accident, someone stumbled into me."

"I know, that's what the witnesses thought, but I saw him. I'm the only one who saw him. If I try and explain it to them it will cause so much fucking aggro. I need to stay here with you, not answer their fucking pointless questions. I've got people on it, the club's called in some favors. We'll take care of it." His hand drifts slowly down the side of my face, a gentle caress.

"Right now, you need sleep. I need you to get better for me. I'll let your mom know you're okay." I look over to the door, half expecting to see her. "She's at home with Elizabeth, don't worry. She didn't think you'd want your girl to see you like this."

I look down at myself, understanding. I can't see my face right now, but what I can see of my body is bruised and battered, numerous grazes and ugly purple and yellow contusions. He's right; I don't want Elizabeth seeing me like this.

Gabe holds my face with both hands, placing the lightest of kisses on my lips. I don't want light, I want Gabe to give me one of his deep, toe curling kisses, but I guess he doesn't feel like that anymore. Not after what I've done to him, losing our baby.

He sits by my side, holding my hand in his, and stays like that until I finally drift off to sleep.

Chapter Eight

Eve

I open my eyes slowly to see Gabe sitting at the end of the bed. He's still in his leathers. His dark blonde hair is messy from raking his hands through it so many times. I look around the bright, clinical room, it's plain and boring and it makes me groan, still in the hospital I see. I must have fallen asleep again because my head is still a throbbing mess. Looking at the sad expression in Gabe's crystal blue eyes reminds me why I'm here and what I've lost. What we lost. Holding back my tears I manage a weak smile which he returns. I notice movement out of the corner of my eye. It's Elle, and from the look of it she's just woken up too. Her blonde hair is still tidy, just a little messy on one side where she was leaning on the arm of the chair, her green eyes are red rimmed and she has a cute little crease on her cheek from sleeping. When she sees that I'm awake her eyes widen. I notice her bottom lip tremble. Gabe gives me a soft kiss, winking at me before getting off the bed. "I'll give you two some time alone."

I nod gratefully, watching as he walks out of the room. That confident swagger of his is so sexy; my eyes gravitate to his firm ass. Damn that man is hot. Here I am looking like a piece of crap lying in this hospital bed. God, I feel so confused! I thought Satan was arrested yet it seems he's free and still wants to kill me, thank fuck he wasn't successful. Then I realize that he killed my unborn baby instead. The baby I didn't even know

I was carrying! I never got the chance to celebrate my pregnancy, that was taken away from me the instant Satan pushed me from the platform.

Elle immediately replaces Gabe on the bed, the door quietly closing behind him. Elle looks me right in the eye. "How are you feeling?" She curses, smacking her palm on her forehead. "How stupid am I? That's the worst question I can ask!"

I reach over, grabbing onto her hand. It's small like mine, fitting perfectly in my grasp. "I'm ok, sad, a little confused, but I'm doing ok. All things considered." I smile and she manages to give me one back, her green eyes sparkling from the tears she's trying to hide from me. She cuddles up to my side as I ask her to tell me all about her shortened trip to London, and how the fuck she ended up with Gabe and the guys. She knows I need a distraction so starts talking, filling me in on everything I've missed, and I'm grateful.

Gabe returns to find us like this, cuddled on the hospital bed, sharing stories. Currently she's grilling me about Ink. It seems they've really hit it off since they met. I love them both, but Ink isn't a settling down kind of guy so I'm a little worried for her. Saying that; Gabe isn't either.

Ink and Cowboy follow Gabe into the room and we stop talking, smiling a greeting at them. Gabe comes straight to my other side, grabbing hold of my hand, as though he's hated every second away from me. He leans forward, planting a soft kiss on my cheek. I'm so glad he's here. I notice Ink's eyes move from me to linger on my friend Elle. I look at Elle and see she's blushing. I hide my smirk as best as I can as Cowboy and Gabe talk. I overhear them saying that Teresa's doing a lot better now. I'm glad to hear it, Gabe had filled me in on how distraught she was, and how worried Prez was for me. Now she knows I'm safe and have Gabe by my side it seems to have calmed her. Not just her though. I feel a sense of calm now he's back with me. I don't know what's going to happen, although I have a sneaky suspicion I know what he's thinking.

After the conversation has stopped, I notice Ink and Cowboy look a little uncomfortable in here. I don't blame them. I decide to give them a helping hand. "Hey guys, you don't have to stay. If you don't mind I'd like some alone time with Angel anyway."

They nod eagerly, Ink flashing me one of his cute winks. Cowboy carefully approaches the bed, lifting my head gently, he kisses my forehead. "Get some rest, sweetheart."

"I will." I whisper back.

Ink approaches next. I feel Gabe's hand tense as it's wrapped around mine. Ink kisses my forehead softly, just like Cowboy. As he pulls back his dark eyes are shining with mischief, something I've missed seeing in my friend. "You still look gorgeous, babe."

I hear a growl from Gabe and Ink gives me another wink which makes me laugh. This earns him a glare from Gabe. I can see Elle trying to hide a laugh behind her hand. When Ink leaves my side, Elle replaces him. "I'd better get going anyway. You want me to check in on Elizabeth for you?"

I let out a sigh. "Yes please, if that's ok?"

She rolls her eyes. "I offered, Eve."

She gives me a cuddle, when she straightens up Ink instantly appears at her side. "I can take you. That's where we're going anyway."
She nods shyly. I turn to Gabe. "They are?"

His face turns serious. "Yeah, I want them looking out for Elizabeth."

I look down at my hands. I hate all of this shit. I don't want anything to happen to my baby, I want her here with me, but I don't want her seeing me like this. I hear Elle say goodbye as she leaves with Ink and Cowboy. Gabe gets out of the chair he was sitting in to snuggle on the bed beside me. One of his legs dangles over the side, there's hardly any room. I doubt he's comfortable, but I sense he needs me as much as I need him right now. He holds me as my tears begin to fall. My head is a mess of emotions. I'm scared, grieving for what I have lost. I'm worried for Elizabeth's safety, yet I'm ecstatic to have Gabe back with me. Gabe softly strokes my hair. I close my eyes, enjoying how good it feels. "Talk to me."

I open my eyes, looking straight into his intense blue ones. "I don't know what to do, Gabe."

I feel my lip tremble and when he notices it, he holds me just a little bit tighter. "I'm here for you now baby, nothing is gonna happen while I'm here. Not to you or to Elizabeth."

I gather myself together, halting my tears. "I didn't know." I whisper.

"I know you didn't, but you can talk to me."

I look up at his face, his beautiful, handsome face. He really is gorgeous. His dark blonde hair, bright sparkling blue eyes and hint of stubble make him look manly and rugged. "Would you have wanted the baby?"

His look hardens and I'm scared to hear his answer. I know I would have wanted to keep it. "Anything that was part of you, I would treasure for a lifetime." His words make my heart beat like crazy. He may be a tough ass biker, but his words are beautiful. "I would have wanted that baby more than anything, Eve. The four of us would have been a family. I'm sorry this has happened, but I promise you I'll make sure Satan pays for this." He looks me right in the eye. "There's plenty of time to make babies, Eve, and we will, but right now I want you to get better so we can go get our girl and go back home."

"What?" His last sentence leaves me confused and speechless. One, he wants more babies. Two, he called Elizabeth our girl which sent butterflies through me, and three he said we're going home but I know he's not talking about a home here in the UK.

"You and Elizabeth are coming back with me." He says it so simply, it's a statement, not a request.

"Gabe, I can't. We have a life here. I can't just move us to Australia."

He places his hand on my cheek, his gaze softening. "Eve, I want you both to be safe. You'll be protected at Severed. Satan is still looking for you, look what he's done to you. What if hurting you isn't enough?"

His words make me tense, a sickening feeling taking hold of me. I thought I was free from all of this. I came home because I thought I was safe. If I'd known I wouldn't have come back and put my daughter in danger. Now there's a chance that I have. Inks words echo through me. "That's why Ink and Cowboy have gone to my house?"

Gabe nods. "She needs protecting too." Oh God. My heart skips a beat. "He's been watching you, Eve. He knows where you live, and he'll have seen Elizabeth."
My heart starts beating frantically. No, not my baby! I hold on to Gabe more tightly. "I'll come back with you, anything to keep Elizabeth safe."

Gabe stares back at me, long and hard. Finally, a relieved look crosses his face. I feel some of the tension release from his body. "I don't want you to come back just for your safety. I want you, Eve. I want everything, you, Elizabeth, a family. I want you back in my life. I want you as my old lady."

I don't have any words. My eyes are wide. I don't realize I'm crying happy tears until Gabe swipes them away with his thumbs. He tucks my head under his chin as my tears start to slow. I think I'm just so relieved and happy. It's scary thinking about moving so far away, but I need to do this. I need to do it for the sake of mine and Elizabeth's safety. And because, if I'm honest with myself, I love Gabe. I've only been away from him for about two days and I craved him so badly. I want to be in his life, I need him. "I love you." I whisper.

He makes a grunting sound. "I love you too. Does that mean your answer's yes?"

I manage a small giggle. "Well I hadn't realised you were asking me, I thought you were telling me, but yes." I pause. "Well, at least until my visa runs out anyway. We'll have to get a visa for Elizabeth too." My face falls as I realize at best we'll only have a few short months together.

"Thank fuck." Gabe lets out a sigh of relief. "We'll sort out the visas expiring once we're home." I get a warm feeling hearing Gabe say the word home, it's more than just four letters when he says it, it's a promise of a future together.

Gabe tells me they're going to release me shortly. As soon as I'm released we're going straight home to pack everything. He wants to meet his girl, and we'll all be leaving together. I can't believe this is happening! I snuggle closer to him, and we just lay there, content to hold each other quietly until I fall asleep again.

Later when I wake up, Gabe wants to talk about our friends. "So, I think Ink likes your friend."

"Elle?" He nods. "Yeah well, I think she more than likes Ink. Did you see her blush?" I laugh.

"They seem to have hit it off." Gabe adds.

"He'd better not hurt her." I point my finger at Gabe.

Gabe smirks. "Babe, the man's a free agent. I ain't getting into his shit. Leave them alone."

I huff and cross my arms in answer. I know he's right. Elle's a grown woman, capable of making her own decisions. I just don't want to see her get hurt or for her not to want to see me again.

Gabe

Eve falls asleep not long after we've talked about her and Elizabeth leaving with me. I can't help but look at her; she looks so peaceful while she sleeps. The troubled expression on her face disappears as she dreams. I need to get her back home with me as soon as possible. I don't like sitting around like this, especially with Elizabeth at home without us.

I had to tell Eve how I felt. I was worried she thought the only reason I wanted her to come back was for her safety. I was right. She was thinking that. When I told her I wanted her, her tears turned to happy ones. She had to know how badly I want her back. I never thought I'd need another person in my life like this, but I do. Eve is my woman. I won't let any harm come to her or Elizabeth.

I slip my arm from under her carefully, sitting up against the end of the bed. I've been terrified that I'd hurt her bruised, fragile body. Seeing her fall was one of the worst things I've ever witnessed. I never want to feel that scared again. I need to get them both out of this country and back to the safety of Severed and my brothers.

I get my phone out, texting Cowboy for an update. I know not to text Ink, that horny fucker will be trying to get in Elle's knickers. If I know him as well as I think I do, he'll have gone off somewhere with her, itching to get his dick wet.

Cowboy texts back that all is well; relieved I lay back down beside Eve, drawing her back into the safety of my arms.

Chapter Nine

Elle

After spending some precious time with Elizabeth, I know I'm going to miss her. She's such an adorable little girl. She's quite intelligent for her age, and the resemblance to her mother is spooky, with her brown wavy hair, bright blue eyes and fair skin. Aside from the usual two year old pronunciation it felt like I was in the room with Eve at times. I think Eve's done a remarkable job of bringing her up. Eve's mother isn't what I was expecting; she seems too young to be a grandmother yet. It's obvious she's besotted by her granddaughter, and the feeling appears to be mutual.

Cowboy took Elizabeth outside to play so Ink and I could talk to Eve's mum. Ink explained that he and Cowboy were going to stay at the house with them, to ensure both their safety whilst Satan is still on the loose.

"What happens when you catch the evil little shit?" she asks, I have to hide my smile as it sounds so wrong, hearing her swearing, but the determined look on her face tells me this was a mama lion and no one is getting close to her cubs.

"We'll take care of It, permanently," Ink assures her. "The less you know the better, but I promise you, when we take care of it, you'll never need to worry again." The words left unsaid speak volumes, we all know it means a death sentence for Satan, but how can any of us feel any guilt or remorse after the evil he's perpetrated in just the past few weeks. Lives taken, lives destroyed and hearts broken. It's the only way forward.

"He'll be wanting to take my girls back with him to Australia then?" she looks more resigned than disappointed. "I'm guessing they'll be safer out there with you lot."

Ink moves across the room, wrapping his strong arms around her and hugging her. This small gesture of affection from the big guy just makes me want him even more. It shows there's a soft side under the steel muscles and tattoos. "She's part of our family now, I know we haven't known her long, but everyone loves her, and we always take care of our own."

Elizabeth comes speeding into the room, giggling like crazy, a flustered looking Cowboy in her wake. This is definitely a guy who's not used to being around children. She's been running rings round him from the look of it, his cheeks are bright red from the fresh breeze outside, but he's sporting a huge grin.

"I beated you Uncle Cowboy" she laughs, running straight for him and launching herself into his arms. He catches her effortlessly, swinging her around so her tiny denim clad legs sweep the room. No need to worry about how Elizabeth will take the move then.

"I'd better call a taxi, I could do to get back to my hotel and have a rest before I pass out", I've barely slept the past twenty four hours, worried about my friend.
"I'll ring it; I'm going to come back with you. I don't want you out there on your own." Ink states, looking to Cowboy for his agreement.

"No worries bro" Cowboy smiles, "I'll take care of our girl here." Elizabeth giggles in his arms, glad that she gets to keep her new playmate a little longer. Ink gestures to Cowboy, who gently places Elizabeth back on the ground and promises to be back in a minute. They both head outside, they've obviously got stuff they need to talk about.

I crouch down in front of Elizabeth; she is such a cute little girl. "Right my darling, I'm going to get going now."

She hugs a koala teddy bear she's just picked up, smiling up at me. "Ok, Elle. Is my mummy coming home now?"

My heart breaks a little for this girl. Her mummy won't be coming home tonight. No little girl should see her mum like that in the hospital. Eve looks pretty bad right now. "I think she's having a sleep over, sweetie." I see her face drop a little. "How about you and Cowboy do lots of fun things together, then when you see your mummy tomorrow you can tell her about it." Her face breaks out in a huge smile and she nods her head quickly, running off in search of Eve's mother and shouting something about baking cookies for Uncle Cowboy.

I shout goodbye again and leave the house smiling, that girl is so sweet. As I step out I see Cowboy and Ink standing by the road. People passing by look at them with wariness, some girls at the end of the street huddle and stare. I can feel lust oozing from them. I make my way over to them while shaking my head, pathetic. Seeing me, Ink steps away from the roadside; giving me a smile that brings me out in shivers. Damn this man is dangerous; he's the embodiment of my every weakness, and everything I should avoid. He's a player, there's no denying that, then again what's the harm in having a little fun?

"You ready for your ride to the hotel?" Ink asks as I move to stand by him, he's gesturing to a taxi just turning the corner into the street. I look to Cowboy who is leaning casually against the garden wall. I wonder why he's called Cowboy. He doesn't seem to have a southern accent and he certainly doesn't wear a cowboy hat.

"Have you let Angel know that Elizabeth is fine? Eve will want to know."

He smiles at me as he gestures at his phone. "Already have."

The sound of a car door opening startles me. I turn to see Ink holding the door of the taxi for me. He inclines his head for me to get in and I see a hint of a scripted tattoo near his neck. I just want to rip his clothes off and find out for myself how many tattoos he has on that fine body of his. He gets in the back of the car, sitting next to me and pulling me close into his side, wrapping his arm around me. I can't help myself, my arms slide underneath his leather jacket. I can feel the defined lines of his muscles under his thin cotton t-shirt. As the taxi pulls away Cowboy raises his hand in a wave, but we've already rounded the bend in the road, too late for me to give him one back in return.

Ink squeezes my shoulder, and with my head resting on the logo of his biker cut, I relax and enjoy the journey to my hotel.

When we pull up in front of the hotel Ink helps me out of the car. He grins as his eyes rake up and down my body and I warm in response.

"So, you gonna invite me up?"
"Erm, I....Sure." I stumble out.

We walk through the hotel lobby together, ignoring the curious looks. I hate that people judge a person just on their appearance. As we walk silently to the elevator I look at him from the corner of my eye, catching him doing the same to me. This makes me laugh. Ink flashes me a cheeky smile. Fuck me, he has a gorgeous smile! It reaches up to his eyes, creating two deep, adorable dimples! Shit, I'm a sucker for a smile and dimples. Team those up with the tattoos, handsome face, dark features and not forgetting his leather and a Harley, it makes for a fucking hot, sexy biker. Who from the look of it can see this for himself. He knows the effect he has on women, and thereby me, and that's a problem. I want him, badly. I need to know what he looks like under his clothing. As we stand side by side in the elevator, Ink's hand wanders up to play with a strand of my hair. It causes shivers to run through me, I love my hair being played with; amongst other things. As he continues to twirl my hair around his thick finger, I begin to imagine how far those tattoos go, where they travel to. Shit, he's coming to my room, where there's a bed, that I so badly want him to throw me on.

He follows me into my room. I can feel his gaze burning into me from behind. I have to bite onto my bottom lip to keep me from groaning. We enter the basic room and I place my bag on the side. I didn't have time to pick out a fancy hotel before I got here. I just went for a great deal, clicked book and hoped for the best. I hated bringing all the luggage here before we could follow Angel to the hospital; luckily it's close to the station, so it was a case of checking in, dumping all our bags and grabbing a taxi. This is the first time I've been back.

"I'm glad that Eve is OK." I say, checking my phone for any messages.

I hear a grunt from behind me and see Ink sitting on the edge of the bed. "We just need to get her back to Severed. Until then she isn't safe, and neither is her daughter."

I gasp. "You really think he would go after a baby?" I'd thought Cowboy staying with Elizabeth was just to reassure Eve, not because there was a real threat.

Ink nods, a huge scowl on his face. It's obvious how much he cares for Eve. I wish I had loyal friends like that. "Satan isn't satisfied with just hurting women, he wouldn't think twice about hurting a child if it meant getting his end result. He's a sick fuck, Elle."

I sigh long and hard, worried for my friend and her sweet little daughter. Just the thought of that man getting his hands on either of them makes my blood boil.

To take my mind off things for a while, Ink decides to order room service. I could say I'm shocked when a whole load of food gets delivered but to be honest I'm not. A man built like Ink obviously has a healthy appetite; I hope it's not just for food!

While we're eating talk turns to my travels and why I love them so much. Not only is it a part of my job, but I just love the life, although I'm getting a little tired of moving from place to place. Meeting Eve makes me wish I had this group of friends for myself. I miss the sense of family, having a place where I belong. I've never really had that. I tell Ink that my next stops are going to be Newcastle and Edinburgh. I've heard good things about them, especially whilst I was in London. I see a spark of interest in Ink's eyes as I talk about going there and what I plan to do whilst I'm there. "Have you travelled far before?" I ask him.

"No, coming here is the first place I've ever flown to. Never been on a plane, never had the need to. I love my home and my club, but hearing you talk about traveling and how excited you are about it when you get there, I dunno. It makes me wish I was coming."

I tilt my head to the side, looking him over. "Why don't you?"

He looks shocked, to be honest, so am I. "You want me to come with you?"

I swallow hard. "Why not? I'm going back to Australia when I'm done there."

He looks thoughtful for a minute and I think he's going to turn me down. "Alright; as long as Angel agrees you're on. Eve's safe, Angel already has their tickets booked. Sure, I'll come."

My heart literally misses a beat. Shit, he shouldn't be affecting me like this already!

"Besides." He adds. "A gorgeous woman like you shouldn't be all alone. You need someone to look after you."

His eyes burn into mine. Oh yeah, I have something he needs to look after right now. Ink licks his lips as he stands. He slowly walks to stand right in front of me as I'm sitting on the edge of the bed. "We can have some fun on this little visit, Elle."

I let my eyes travel all the way up his body, from his high leather boots to his sexy fucking face. On my way up I notice there's a healthy sized bulge hiding in his jeans. I get the feeling I'm going to get to get a good look at what's causing that bulge. "What sort of fun?" I tease.

I see his jaw tense as he reaches forward to grab hold of my hand. He yanks me up, I crash into his hard chest. I don't even have time to think before his lips are all over mine, claiming me. My lips surrender to his and we kiss, my hands start to reach up to his neck, but his hands wrap around both of mine, grasping them and forcing them behind my back. I gasp into his mouth and Ink growls in return. "Undress," He commands. He lets me go and I stare at him as he backs away, watching me. He takes off his leather jacket, placing it over a chair in the corner. He never takes his eyes off me. His black t-shirt is short sleeved, revealing swirling tattoos covering his arms. They are kind of hypnotic as I stare at them. "What's the matter, Elle?" Ink asks in his deep voice.

"Nothing," I squeak.

He crosses his arms in front of his chest. "Then undress for me babe."

I slowly unbutton my jeans, bending over at the waist as I drag them down to my ankles, ripping them off and revealing my skimpy black lace panties. His eyes burn into me as I straighten myself. I reach for the hem of my plain shirt, pulling it over my head. As my hair falls back into place I hear a groan from Ink. Pure female satisfaction fills me as I watch him take in my elegant lingerie. I love my matching sets; I don't feel properly dressed without them.

"Fuck, Elle." He growls, taking a step closer to me. I reach my fingers into the top of my panties, about to pull them down and bare myself for the man in front of me, but Ink stops me. "No, let me do that." He pushes me down to sit on the bed, telling me to scoot back, so I'm sitting right at the far end, next to the pillows.

Ink begins to undress by the end of the bed, eyes burning into mine as he removes his boots. He rips off his belt and yanks down his jeans before pulling his shirt off over his head. Oh my. Ink, shirtless! Damn! I feel my panties begin to dampen as my arousal increases. Not only are his arms covered in tattoos, but so is his chest. Fuck, Ink is so fucking sexy. I see the bulge barely hidden in his black boxers, licking my lips in anticipation. Seeing this Ink lowers them, quickly moving up onto the bed. He kneels in front of me, my eyes greedily taking him in. He has a nipple ring, I'm eager to take it in my mouth and pull on it, but first my eyes want to take him all in while he's this close. My eyes stop on his impressive package. Fuck, Ink is huge. I've been with a few men but none of them compared to Ink in size. Is that even going to fit inside me? I mean Jesus, Ink has a big dick! Not only that, I whimper as I notice the man's pierced! He has his cock pierced! There are two silver balls, both under and on top of his tip, and there are more, continuing down his cock like a ladder. Fuck, what the hell will they feel like? My eyes widen and I hear Ink laugh. My eyes snap to his, shit there's those damned dimples again. "You like my piercings?"

All I can manage is a quick nod of my head. Ink leans in closer. "I've heard they feel really good when they're inside you."

I take in a sharp breath. I want to know what they feel like. He looks unbelievably hot right now, kneeling in front of me. Naked, tattoos on show, abs to die for and his hard, pierced cock pointing right at me. Ink is downright sexy and dangerous. His body demanding pleasure I'm eager to give to him.

I reach forward, grasping his hard cock. The balls feel odd under my touch, but I pull on it anyway. Ink's eyes close a little, his hiss letting me know he likes it. I need to taste him. Before I can begin to move, to take him in my mouth and pleasure him, Ink leans close, removing my bra with little effort at all. My breasts are exposed. He takes a long hard look before taking a nipple in his mouth, licking and sucking, sending pleasure shooting between my legs. I lean back down on the soft bed. I feel Ink's hand trail down my body. When he gets to my thin panties, he tugs hard, ripping them away from my body. A growl comes from Ink and he sucks a little harder, biting on my nipple. I gasp, this feels so good.

Ink's hand covers my wet pussy. He presses his palm down, making circular movements right on my clit, his fingers moving in an up and down motion. My legs open wider. I moan as he kisses me again. "So wet for me." Ink growls against my mouth. I feel an orgasm coming on. No! I don't want to come yet, I want this feeling to last.

"Don't hold it back. Let me make you come, all over my hand." At his words I fall into my orgasm. My lips separate from his, my head falling back onto the pillow. Moaning as I release.

When I open my eyes, Ink is looking down at me, licking his fingers. "That was fucking hot babe."

He moves from the bed to pick up his jeans. I lay still, shattered and unable to move from my orgasm. He returns with a condom wrapper, tears it with his teeth then sheaths himself. "Now for the good bit."

Quickly I'm spun around; I'm lying on my front. Ink's hands grip under my hips, tilting my ass up. I gasp as I hear a loud slap, feeling a sting on my behind. He slapped me! No sooner have I thought it when another slap comes down on my other cheek. This one, however, making me gasp with pleasure. I get even wetter; I'm definitely ready for another round. His sheathed, pierced cock springs to mind and I push my ass back on him. I want him in me, now. "Greedy girl," He says, spanking me hard again. I sigh blissfully as he rubs his hands gently over my ass, soothing the pain. I never thought I'd enjoy this, but I do. I fucking love him spanking me! Ink grips me again, pulling me up against him, my ass high in the air as he drives his cock home. My head falls back, my hair falling down my back as Ink thrusts into me, again and again. Those pierced balls are hitting just the right spot to make me scream. Ink's hands dig in harder, I grip more tightly on the sheets and Ink brings his hand down on me again. Smacking me so hard it brings tears to my eyes, but I fucking want more. "Oh, god!"

"That's it baby. Come for me. Scream for me."

Ink thrusts in, hard, tilting his hips to the side a little so his cock hits a different spot. My eyes roll back in pleasure. This is almost too much to handle. I've never climaxed during penetration before; this feeling is foreign to me. His cock thrusts hard inside of me, and I let go. I scream his name, digging my nails into the bed as I come. It's the most intense feeling I've ever had. I already know I want more. Just as I finish coming down Ink growls one last time, exploding inside of me. I feel his cock thicken as he fills the condom.

Ink gets up after carefully laying me down on the bed. I watch through heavy eyes as he walks into the bathroom. I don't see him come out as exhaustion takes over, and I fall into a deep sleep.

Chapter Ten

Eve

Sitting in the taxi on my way home from the hospital I'm a mix of emotions. I'm grieving for the baby I've sadly lost, I'm scared that Satan is going to try something else before we can get back to the safety of Severed and Angel's club. But, my overriding emotion is joy. Joy because the man sitting next to me is here. He's come to take me home with him, and to claim me as his own.

I wince slightly as the car hits a speed bump in the road at the wrong angle, I hadn't realized just how sore and achy my body still feels after my fall. Angel notices, reaching over to me and drawing me closer into his protective hold. I sigh contentedly, this feels good.

As we pull into the street I can see Elizabeth with her bouncing dark curls as she's jumping up and down in the doorway of the house, a huge grin on her face. I can tell she's giddy with excitement and I know without hearing her that she's making that cute noise she makes when she's so excited. It's half squeal and half giggle, it's an adorable sound. Cowboy has a protective hold on her shoulder until he sees Angel getting out of the car, then let's her loose. As soon as Elizabeth spots me, she comes racing up to me and jumps into my arms. That hurts and I hold in my wince of pain, but it doesn't matter how much it hurts, it feels good to hold my baby girl, to see her safe and to cherish the tiny kisses she's peppering my face with.

Angel comes to my side having paid the taxi driver and retrieved my overnight bag. His face lights up as he sees Elizabeth and she squeals when she spots him. "It's my angel mummy! My angel came to see me!"

Elizabeth starts wriggling and reaching for Angel. He can see I'm struggling and reaches over to take her from my arms. I can't believe how easily she goes to him, it makes my heart swell to see them holding each other. Angel looks at her with such pure adoration, it brings tears to my eyes. Elizabeth starts chattering away so quickly I can't keep track of what she's saying, and she whispers something in Angels ear whilst looking at me. I'm pretty sure I see her mouth the word cake in there.

Cowboy gives me a gentle hug, welcoming me home, then leads me into the house. Closely followed by everyone else. It's crowded in here, I spot Ink and Elle quietly talking to each other, as well as my mother, however I don't recognize the man she's speaking to over in the corner.

Finally noticing me as I walk further into the living room they all come closer and welcome me back. My mother leads the stranger she was talking to over for introductions. "Eve, I'd like you to meet John. He's my friend. He wanted to come meet you before you jet off back to Australia."

I'm pretty sure that I saw my mother just bestow a look of affection on John. I think I'm missing something here from the glances they're sharing with each other. I'm about to talk to John when Elizabeth takes my hand, bouncing up and down at my side."Mummy, mummy I baked you a cake!" She sing songs in her loud, high pitched voice.

She runs off into the kitchen and Elle flashes me a warm smile before following her. When they come out together Elizabeth walks proudly in front of Elle who is holding a very lopsided cake with childish decorations on it. Looking closely I think they're possibly stick figures drawn on with colored icing. "What a beautiful cake, baby girl. Did you make it?" I'm hoping she'll tell me what it's supposed to be rather than making me guess.

"Auntie Elle helped me, but I did the icing all on my own." She quickly speaks, taking a deep breath before continuing. "It's you and me and our angel, Mummy." I smile proudly at my girl. I'm pretty sure that Elizabeth's contribution was more making a mess of the kitchen and licking the spoon rather than the actual baking.

Elizabeth looks up to Angel, grinning widely at him, baby teeth and all. Angel bends down to her level, giving her a kiss on the forehead which makes her giggle. "It's perfect, princess."

Elizabeth looks back to me smiling, I know that she's secretly telling me how much she just loved him calling her that.

Angel seems to sense that I'm feeling weary, so he guides me over to a chair. He sits first, drawing me down onto his lap and holding me close. Drawing me into his warmth, god I've missed this.

We spend the next couple of hours with our friends, chatting about nothing in particular, and especially nothing to do with recent events, I'm grateful for the reprieve.

When everyone's finally left us to it, I ask my mother to come sit down for a chat. I need to explain to her how serious the threat from Satan is, and ask her to come with us to Australia. Angel spends the next hour telling my mother all about Satan. How he contributed to Beth's death several years ago, how he has no compunction about killing, and how dangerous and cold he is.

He makes it perfectly clear that the threat from Satan now includes my mother and Elizabeth. "Mum, you know that Angel's taking me and

Elizabeth back to Australia with him, we'd like you to come with us as well."
I never thought I'd see the day when I asked my mother to go anywhere
with me.

She looks slightly taken aback by my request as well."Eve, I can't just up
and leave my life here". She pauses, she's mulling something over, trying
to decide I think if it's something she wants to share with me. "I wasn't sure
how to tell you about this but I've met someone. I used to know him before
you were born and he's come back into my life recently. He's asked me to
move in with him, and I'm going to."

I'm spluttering like a fish, my mouth opening and closing but no words
come out. My mother hasn't shown interest in a man for as long as I can
remember. In fact she's spent most of my life telling me how useless and
worthless they are, yet her whole face has lit up telling me she's moving in
with her new man. "But... What... Who?" The words come stumbling out.
Angel's watching me, trying not to laugh.

"You met him earlier, his name is John." My mother then shares her story
with us.

She'd met John long before she met my father and they'd fallen in love.
John didn't meet my grandfathers expectations so he'd forbidden my Mum
from seeing John. Being young and in love they didn't listen, and carried on
seeing each other behind my grandfathers back. When he found out my
grandfather was furious and he moved my mother and the rest of the family
away. Her father then Introduced her to my Dad, one of his new work
colleagues. Sadly, my Dad wasn't the man my Grandfather thought he
was. Once he had slept with my mum he dropped her, not wanting the
complication of a pregnancy when she told him about it. Grandfather had
been so disgusted by her behavior that he'd ostracized her from the family,
and John had already moved away so my mother never saw him again.
This was why she hated men, in her eyes they'd all let her down. This

turned her into a sour woman, making her the mother who had raised me. Then John had shown up at the door one day having finally tracked her down. It sounded like something out of one of the books I read. But for the first time I can remember my mum looks happy.

Right now though my mother's happiness isn't my main concern, her safety is. With a sleeping Elizabeth in my arms, I turn to Angel. "Is it safe to leave mum here?"

"I'm not sure, babe. I'm guessing he'll follow us as soon as he realizes we're leaving. He's hell bent on hurting you. But," he pauses, not quite sure how to phrase the next words I guess. "I can't promise he won't try and hurt your mum just to hurt you."

"Eve, I've waited half my life to find John again. I'm not leaving now, just because some thug might or might not, come after me. I'll just take him up on his offer to move in with him. He'll look after me."

My mum always has been stubborn, choosing to do what she wants over and above what I might want, but I guess I can't begrudge her this opportunity for love. Not when I've just found my perfect man.

We spend the next half hour or so finding out more about John, and how important he is to my mum when we're interrupted by the doorbell. Elle, Ink and Cowboy have returned, baggage and all.

After conferring with the guys, Angel advises me to go start packing. "Only bring the essentials babe, we'll get whatever else you need once we're home. The tickets are sorted and we have to leave soon."

I can feel myself go white, the shock of what we're doing starting to hit me. I'm moving halfway across the world to be with this man I hardly know, and I've only got a few hours to pack my life up. I giggle nervously as I realize that I don't have a real life here other than Elizabeth anyway. I'm working in a dead end job, I'm living back with my mother, and the only light in my life is my daughter. There's nothing here I'm going to miss. In Australia I'll have my best friend, my hot man, and the guys who've come to treat me like family already. I can't wait for Elizabeth to meet everyone.

With that thought, I carefully place Elizabeth down on the sofa and head upstairs to pack.

***

Satan

I'm fucking furious! I watched that bitch and her daughter leave earlier with Angel and his cohorts. They had a couple of suitcases with them and from what I could overhear he's taking her back to Severed. Granted it will be a lot easier for me if she's back in Australia, I don't have the contacts here, or the resources I have back home. I'm not rushing after them though, I've one last thing to do for Eve before I head home.

The light in the front room goes out. I'll give the old cow an hour or so to fall asleep before I go in.

I spend the hour imagining all the things I'll do to Eve when I get hold of her. If Angel thought I hurt Beth, that's nothing to what I plan to do to his latest bitch. Before she dies I'll make sure it's my name she's fucking screaming as I take her, not his.

The house is silent, as are the neighboring houses as I make my way through the shadows, supplies in hand. I reach the front door, pushing the petrol soaked rags through the letterbox, followed by the lighter. I move round to the back of the house, breaking the glass on the rear door, and pushing more petrol soaked rags through the hole. I can smell the smoke already. I retreat to the safety of the shadows in the front of the house, settling in to watch the carnage unfold. This should put me in a good mood for the journey back home.

I grin in satisfaction, watching the flames devour the old house. I've unleashed the fires from hell, my only regret is that Eve isn't in there along with her mother. I'm disappointed I can't hear the old cow screaming though, or see her trying to escape. It would have been nice to see her struggle before she died, I guess the smoke took her out early on. Still, I've got the satisfaction of watching the roof collapse in before the fire engines finally make their way into the street. Such a shame they'd been called away on a false alarm in the opposite direction just before I lit this fire. They might have been able to save the old cow, who's probably nothing more than ashes now, just like her house.

***

Gabe

We've been on this plane for four hours now and I'm already wishing the flight was over. I fucking hate these long haul flights. I'll be glad when we finally touchdown in Australia, and I can get my girls to safety.

Eve shifts and I watch her cautiously. She still looks battered and bruised. She needs all the rest she can get after her recent ordeal. Both her and Elizabeth quickly fell asleep when the plane took to the sky. I'm so glad to have her close to me again. I can finally breathe easy. Knowing she was in serious danger and so far away was fucking scary. I never want to experience anything like that again. I smooth down her soft hair and ease her back to sleep. I look down at her shirt covering her stomach and think of what could have been. I can't believe that she had my baby inside her.

Essentially my brother not only injured my woman, but he killed our unborn child! That makes me hate the fucker even more.

I bite down on my teeth, my hands balling into fists as the hate flows through me.

"Angel." A very sleepy voice murmurs my name. I turn towards it; Elizabeth is looking at me from Cowboys lap, a big smile on her face. With Eve asleep, she decided to crawl onto Cowboys lap and snuggle to sleep on him. I won't lie and say it didn't disappoint me a little; I wanted her to come to me.

Her bright smile is directed at me, immediately calming me down. Just like that, my anger is forgotten. She looks up at a sleeping Cowboy, giggling at his quiet snoring, and then reaches her arms out to me. My heart leaps out of my chest as I quickly move to lift her onto my lap. Cowboy's arms tighten around her and his eyes open. He's on high alert. It's both funny and admirable.

"It's ok brother, I got her."

He relaxes, falling right back to sleep. Once she's snuggled into me, Elizabeth looks up at me and her eyes sparkle. She reaches her chubby little hand up to pinch my nose. I pretend that it hurts, earning one of her precious laughs. She repeats the action and I pretend it hurts again.

"Ouch!"

Elizabeth breaks out in giggles causing Eve to stir in her sleep. I look at Eve and smile. Elizabeth pokes me with her finger, making a quiet motion with a finger to her lips. "Shh."

I nod my head. "Mummy needs her sleep."

Elizabeth nods her head, leaning over to Eve to plant a soft kiss on her mother's hair. "Night, night, mummy."

This girl is so fucking adorable. She already has me and Cowboy falling at her feet, no doubt the rest of the club will react in exactly the same way. In this moment I know that I will do anything it takes to keep both my girls safe, from everything, and everyone. I also know that Elizabeth will grow up loved by the club, she will be our own little princess biker. That makes me laugh. Elizabeth looks up at me. Her eyes look sleepy again. This girl loves her damn sleep.

She wedges herself in between the arm I have around Eve and myself. It's a little awkward, no doubt my arm will be numb when I wake, regardless I let her fall asleep and I quickly follow her.

Chapter Eleven

Gabe

I'm so fucking relieved to finally be setting foot back in the clubhouse. The weather doesn't hurt either. I stand in the doorway and look around as Eve steps in beside me, followed by Cowboy. It feels like a lifetime ago since I left here to go find Eve, and part of me still can't believe she's back here at my side. Teresa rushes towards us, screeching Eve's name, pulling her into her arms. We haven't told her what's been happening over in England yet. I cradle Elizabeth tighter in my arms, she's slept all the way back from the airport, too excited to sleep on the plane. As I look down at her sleeping face a warm buzz goes through my body. This little beauty is part of my family now; I'll protect her and Eve with my life.

Some of the brothers and old ladies are hugging Eve and cooing over Elizabeth's form in my arms. It's Diane who thankfully brings some order to the chaos. "Come on guys; give the girl some room to breathe. She looks shattered. You need to go sleep sweetie." She tells Eve, who gratefully gives her a tired smile. "I put a cot bed in your room Angel; figured Eve would want her girl close to her." I thank Diane, and mutter a few words of greeting to the brothers as I take my tired girls and lead them to my room.

Eve collapses on the bed, the exhaustion clear on her face, the bruising still showing vivid purple and yellow around her eye. Her face is pale, highlighting the hurt she's suffered. I want to hold her in my arms and tell her it's going to be okay while I make gentle love to her, but I'm scared of hurting her after what she's been through. I need to stop being a selfish fucker, worrying about what I want, and give her some space to heal. But looking at my beautiful woman undressing, after worrying about her and missing her, I just want to rip her clothes off and fill her with my cock. Elizabeth stirs in my arms bringing me back to reality.

I walk over to the cot bed that Diane set up and place a sleeping Elizabeth down, laying a light sheet over her to keep off any chill. She's shown such trust in me from the moment we met. I plant a kiss on her chubby cheek and I vow to this little girl that I'll keep her and her mother safe and love her till the day I die. She's my daughter now, and being the VP's daughter makes her precious property.

I sit in the chair in the corner of the room, content just to watch my girls sleeping for now. It feels good to have them here finally. Once we've sorted out the threat from Satan I can't wait to buy us a proper home, with a garden for Elizabeth to play in, a swing set for me to push her in, and a kick ass king size bed to honor and worship her mother in and make Elizabeth some brothers to watch over her.

There's a gentle knock at the door, before I can stand, it opens slightly and Prez pops his head around. "Angel, there's a call from England for Eve, I don't want to wake her but I think you'd better come take it, it sounds serious."

What's the fucker done now? I rise from the chair, check on Elizabeth and brush her hair gently back from her forehead before following Prez back down to his office.

***

I can't believe the call I've just taken. Satan burned down Eve's mother's house! The sick fucker. The only good news is that Eve's mother was out when it happened. I guess he hadn't expected her to be sleeping over at her boyfriends that night. I tried to persuade her to come out and stay with us, even if it was just for a short stay, I'm worried what the news will do to Eve. I know she's not that close to her mum, but they do seem to have made some progress in their relationship of late from what she's told me.

Prez is contacting the UK chapter of Runaway to see if they have any news on Satan. They've not been much help, they're clubhouse is situated too far away really. By the time they were able to make it to York most of the action was over, although they've agreed to keep someone close to watch over Eve's mum.

Ink didn't come back with us; he's gone off on some sort of road trip with the travel reporter he met. I doubt there'll be much sight-seeing done other than a hotel room bed. Lucky bastard. I can't say I'm sorry he's in a different country to Eve right now, I'm a jealous fucker and I didn't like how close he was to Eve when she was out here before. So if he's into this blonde chick, I'm all fucking for it.

Prez has told me to leave plans to him for now, he's put the word out and we've got plenty of people looking out for Satan coming back into the country. I just wish I knew how he found out the details of Eve's flight. As far as I knew the only people who had that information were here in the clubhouse, and I don't like the bitter taste that leaves in my mouth. That would mean one of my brothers had betrayed her. I don't want to believe it, but right now, I can't think of any other explanation. I've clued Prez into my suspicions, and for now we're keeping it to ourselves but watching everyone closely.

I head back to my room, my girls are still sleeping. I lay down on the bed beside Eve, drawing her into my arms and decide to rest my eyes for a few minutes.

***

Elle

I step off the train onto the platform at Newcastle station. These English stations are beautiful, large arched roofs, brick walls, and an antique feel to them. I think I read somewhere they were built by the Victorians. Ink follows me, not bothering to look around at the building like I have. Both of our bags in his hands, but it doesn't stop him catching a quick grope of my backside. The man is insatiable and I love it. He's also absolutely amazing in bed and his magical piercings are a bonus. I can't remember the last time I had so much sex, and it's never been as good as it is with him.

I'm a realist, he's not the settling down type, so I'm going to use him and abuse him for my own needs whilst he's here. It would be rude not to! Besides, he's most definitely thinking the exact same thing.

Ink looks with disgust at the automated ticket barrier, then down at the ticket in his hand. I can't help but laugh at him, taking the ticket and putting it in the slot for him so he can move through. We're staying in the hotel across the road from the station. It's another grand old building, they've got large rooms, big beds and it's within walking distance of all the pubs and stores I want to visit on this leg of my journey.

Right now my priority is a hot shower, preferably sharing it with Ink. So that means a long, hot, sexy shower. By then I should be able to ring home and check in on Eve, make sure they got back okay, and see how she's feeling after her accident.

I laugh at the look the staid and proper receptionist gives Ink as we approach the desk. He's not this hotel's normal type of clientele, it's a bit classier than the usual stag and hen do market which is why I chose it, it's more suited to the suited and booted business client than this rough and ready biker. He grimaces back at the receptionist, reaching for me and planting a long, heavy kiss on my lips. He's going to cause trouble if I don't hurry up and get him to the room, so I rush through the check in procedure as quickly as I can.

No sooner are we in the lift than Ink reaches for me, his hands caressing up underneath the skirt I am wearing.

As soon as the hotel room door is opened and we're inside Ink drops the bags, and slamming the door shut without taking his eyes from me. He slowly stalks towards me, causing a shiver to run down my spine. Once I'm within his reach he grabs me hard against his body, capturing my lips. He lights a fire within me, it becomes a competition to see who can get the other undressed the quickest as we rip each other's clothes off. When we're both naked, he lifts me, smashing my back against the wall. My legs wrap around him and he slams into me hard, causing me to scream.

"God, I've fucking wanted to be inside you all the way here." He growls, slamming into me once again. As he pounds into me over and over he bites onto my shoulder, that little bit of pain has me spiraling into an orgasm, closely followed by Ink.

He lowers me to my feet, and on shaky legs I head to the bathroom for a nice hot shower. I hear the snap of the condom as Ink sorts himself out. Turning on the water I step into the steamy, hot shower and sigh. Damn that feels good. After washing my hair I turn and see Ink staring at me, watching me, a look of lust in his eyes. He slowly pumps his hard cock as it greedily points at me. Immediately I want him again.

"Let me see you wash those pretty tits of yours." He demands, and I comply.

I gather water, rubbing my breasts as I watch him, watch me. I tug slightly on my nipples, biting my lip to hide my groan. Ink steps into the shower, his dark eyes watching me as I continue to rub on my breasts. He stills my hands and removes them, lowering his head to take my nipple in his mouth. This time I can't hide the groan that escapes. The more his tongue pays attention to my nipple, the more wet I become, and it's not from the shower. I'm hungry for him. With no warning I pull Inks head back, removing his mouth from me. I lower myself to my knees before him, admiring his hard cock. I look up at Ink as I swipe my tongue from balls to tip. Capturing the tip in my mouth as I go, drawing it deeper. Ink lets a moan escape as I suck harder on his tip. I take him in my mouth as deep as I can without gagging, that's no easy task seeing as Ink is a big boy. I do my best though, using my hand to pump the rest of his member. Ink brings his hands into my hair, fucking my mouth as I move my head up and down. Moaning from the excitement as I pleasure him. Suddenly I'm pulled up to stand in front of him; he lifts me under my arms. He kisses me hard as he brings my back to the cold tiled shower wall.

"Condom." He mumbles in between kisses, but he doesn't move.

"Go get it then." I answer back.

A few more deep kisses, a loud groan from Ink and he steps away. Leaving me to go and fetch his condom. I shouldn't bitch about it, at least he's sensible. Me on the other hand, I just want him inside of me as quickly as I can have him. I'm not usually this careless with men, believe me. I'm the crazy girl that's makes sure I'm protected and so is he. I don't want any unexpected surprises, but with Ink, my deepest brain drilled precautions are long forgotten when he gets me worked up.

When I return Ink is still hard and ready for me. I playfully squeal as he turns me around to face the wall, smacking me hard on the ass. That felt painfully good, I push out my bottom waiting for the next slap. He gives it to me harder, causing my pussy to clench in need. "Ink," I growl.

"Spread your legs." He demands. Naturally, I obey. Careful not to slip I brace my hands on the wall. But Ink doesn't fill me, instead he continues to pleasure me with smacks and slaps. They range from the tops of my thighs, to my bottom but then they start to wander to my eager pussy. He slaps my pussy hard; it's both painful and glorious. Never has a man made me feel like this!

When the slaps become too much I grind my ass onto him. "Please Ink, I need you now!"

He ignores me, biting down on my shoulder from behind as he continues to slap my wet pussy. The extra pain brings on my orgasm. I scream my release as it surprises me. I haven't even come down from my high when Ink brings himself home. Slamming into me so hard my orgasm is taken to another level. My mouth hangs open, my eyes rolling to the back of my head in pure ecstasy.

Ink holds tightly onto me, he fucks me hard, the shower still on, washing away our sweat.

"Come for me, Elle."
What? Is he serious right now? I've just come twice, I can't manage a third!

"I can't." I whimper as he thrusts even harder

"Yes, you fucking can." He reaches forward, pinching my hard clit. Circling his fingers, he traps my clit between them. Sure enough, I come hard, it makes me literally weak at the knees. Ink holds me up as he follows, growling in my ear. Fuck me; Ink knows my body better than I do!

After quickly removing the condom, he holds me under the shower whilst we wash ourselves, and then helps me out. We smile stupidly at each other as he towel dries us both, then like the kind biker he only shows to certain people; he carries me to the huge bed. Lying naked next to each other, I fall into a blissful sleep.

***

Gabe

When I wake up its deadly quiet.

I've had a shits night's sleep from fucking worrying about how Eve is going to handle what I have to tell her. Prez thinks I shouldn't tell her after the stress she's had lately, but I have to. I don't want to lie about anything when it comes to Eve, so I know what I have to do.

This is going to really fucking hurt her. I tell you what, I'll be glad to finally be fucking rid of Satan! Ever since I've met Eve we've had him hovering over us. Always there, niggling away in the background.

My fists tighten; he'll never get his hands on my woman.

I hear Elizabeth stir, she wants her juice. I quietly get up from the bed, handing Elizabeth her juice. It's so funny; she doesn't even open her eyes as she holds up her hands for it. She closes her tiny hands around the pink juice bottle, guzzling it down. Now that she's had her juice I know she'll be good for at least another hour. The girl loves her sleep.

With a heavy heart I turn to make my way back to bed. I want to make sure Eve gets as much sleep as she can, or maybe I'm just wimping out on telling her. Only, when I turn around, Eve is looking at me, a big sleepy smile on her face.

"Morning, sweetheart." I get in beside her.

She rolls over, sliding her hand over my exposed chest. "Morning biker."

I laugh at that. Eve slides her hand downwards. I'd love nothing more than to let her grab my dick, but it would lead to sex and it's too soon after her accident, that and I have something to tell her.

I stop her by placing my hand on top of hers. She frowns at me. "Gabe?"

"I need to tell you something."

She searches my face then sits up, looking over at me. Fuck me, she's beautiful. She holds the sheet at her breasts with one hand, but I can see the side of them as they swell. My dick stirs, but I shake the sexual lust from my head. Eve leans on her free hand, looking me right in the eyes, bright blues to mine.
Something's wrong. You have your serious face on."

I manage a small smile. "Yeah babe, it's serious."

She leans in and kisses my chest, easing the confession out of me. I take a deep breath, come on Gabe, you can do this.

"Last night, we had a call from your mother."

Eve's eyes go a little wide but she nods her head for me to continue.

"Eve, your mother's house was burned down the day we left. Your mum wasn't inside, don't worry. She was at her boyfriends, she's safe."

Eve clasps her hand to her chest. "Oh thank god."

Tears gather in her eyes. I lift her head to mine, kissing her softly.

"Why us Gabe? Why is all this shit happening?"

"I don't know, but I promise you I will end this."

"I don't want you to get hurt." She whispers.

"Don't you worry baby, nobody will get to me. But I will protect you and Elizabeth with my life. You hear me?"

She nods, tears falling down her cheeks. I gather her tightly in my arms, whispering comforting words to soothe her as she softly cries.

Chapter Twelve

Elle

This food is truly delicious. While we were walking around Newcastle we were advised to visit the Salsa Cafe tapas bar, and I am so glad we did. The food is great, and there's plenty of it. There's a rustic feel to the building, chunky wooden tables and chairs adding to the atmosphere. It's a little on the dark side, but lights flicker around the restaurant to give it a romantic feel. I'm a little tipsy from the drinks we've had, so when I see Ink has finished his mouthful of food I become brave. Instead of sitting face to face, Ink decided he wanted to sit as close as possible to me. So we're sitting next to each other, partially hidden away in a corner, enjoying our tapas. I lean in close, kissing his stubble, his hand wraps around the back of my head as he turns to face me. He kisses me deeply on the lips and I return it.

He breaks away, giving me a naughty grin as he looks at me. I watch as he gathers a little of the left over bruschetta from the table then orders me to open my mouth. Slipping the food in, he lets his finger enter too. I look him right in the eye as I suckle on his finger as he slowly removes it from my mouth. Wearing a cheeky smile as he watches me eat the delicious food he fed me.

Once I've eaten the food, I decide to reciprocate the gesture, picking up some prawns for Ink. I slip my finger in his mouth as he sucks, and as my finger slides out I have an idea. "Oops, you spilled some."

I lean into him, eyes connecting for just a second before I close them, swiping my tongue slowly along Ink's smooth bottom lip. There's no spilled food at all, I just wanted to taste him. After a very pleasurable night last night in our hotel room, we spent most of today touring the sights of Newcastle. Now we've had time to rest I want him again.

As I lick I feel him tense. When I pull back he's got a very serious look on his face. "Careful sweetheart, a man like me can only take so much from a beauty like you."

I give him a smile. He's forever flattering me, his words leaving me flushed. It's what a charmer does though, that's what I need to remember. No doubt he's said these same words to many other girls before me.

I feed myself some chicken this time, licking my fingers before looking back up at Ink, an innocent look on my face. "I don't know what you're talking about."

Immediately Ink stands, making me jump. He walks over to the bar and I see him hand over some money. I hide my smile as he returns to me. When he reaches me he yanks me up from my seat, holding me against his hard body. "Sweetheart, you just ended this meal with your teasing. We're going to the hotel. Now." With that he pulls me along. "I know just the thing to fill that greedy mouth of yours." He mutters as we leave.

I giggle as he speeds up, not caring about the curious glances from the other diners. I'm having way too much fun.

***

I'm sitting on a hard chair, my breathing shallow. I'm feeling pretty helpless right now. I can't move an inch. My legs are tied to the chair I'm sitting on; my arms are tied and secured behind the back of the chair. I'm completely naked and I can't see a thing. The blindfold covering my eyes makes sure of that. I'm experiencing so much ecstasy that I don't care how naked I am before his eyes.

Ink growls as he settles himself between my quivering thighs. When he tied my legs to the chair, he made sure that they were spread wide for him. I'm on display for his enjoyment, it makes me so horny.

I feel Ink's dark stubble as he scrapes it along the insides of my thighs. He moves his head closer to the magic spot. It's not close enough for me, I almost growl with impatience. Just one single, glorious swipe of his tongue along my quivering wetness has me melting and starting to plead. "Ink!"

I need more, he's been teasing me all fucking day!

This morning we arrived in Edinburgh, spending the day taking in some of the sights. While we were having what was supposed to be an innocent day, Ink being his usual self, turned it into a not so innocent day. All day he's been kissing me on my neck, biting my earlobe, smacking my ass and whispering naughty things in my ear.

When we finally made it back to our hotel room, I was almost horny beyond control. I wanted to jump him and rip off every bit of his clothing; however Ink stopped me as he had ideas of his own.

First he got me naked, slowly, planting soft kisses all over my body along the way. Then he blindfolded me. So here I am, bound and naked before him and I love it! I am in kinky heaven right now!

Ink gives me a few more swipes with that talented tongue of his, then he's gone, leaving me on the edge. He soon comes back though. I can feel him standing beside me, his cock grazing my shoulder. I feel drops of thick liquid drop on my body. It drips between my legs, down my breasts and along my arms and stomach. Ink begins to lick my body, everywhere the drops have touched. I break out in a shiver. The sweet aroma of chocolate reaches my nose. Ink moves his focus to my breasts. He licks everywhere apart from my nipples. I squirm within my bounds as he teases me. I want him to give my nipples the attention they need. After he finishes with my breasts, he travels downwards, licking along the insides of my thighs. He dips a finger inside my mouth; I groan as the chocolate covers my tongue. I almost start pleading again as he continues to tease me. I need him to reach my pussy; but he licks everywhere else instead, I have no doubt that I will come if he does.

When he makes sure I'm clean of all the chocolate, he stands, pulling my head in his direction. He guides his cock into my mouth, it's covered in chocolate. I moan in pleasure at the sweetness, happily licking him clean. It's not enough though, I need to feel him, to touch that fabulous body of his, and I really want to see him, his gorgeous face and those dangerous, sexy tattoos.

I hear Ink's sharp intake of breath as I suck harder. He removes his cock with a pop. I try pleading with him again. "Please, Ink."

This time I get my wish as he gently removes my bindings; only the ones securing my legs though. He guides me to stand and gently moves me to the bed, laying me down and moving me further up the bed. Ink loosens the bind on my wrists, moving my arms so they're above my head. He ties the binding to the bed so I can't move my arms. I feel him hovering over me; then without any warning, he slams into me. I groan loudly at the amazing feeling of him filling every part of me. I'm still not used to his size, the sting only adds to my enjoyment though.

It's not long until the sensations become too much, and I come. Ink continues his thrusts, growling and biting me. His movements cause the pressure to build inside me again. He rips the blindfold from my eyes, after blinking a few times my blurred vision becomes clear and I see him. Ink stares down at me, a dark look in his eyes, he's so fucking hot. If I'm not careful, this man will hurt me; I need to make sure I protect my heart so that doesn't happen. This is just innocent fun for both of us.

Ink kisses me hard, and I whimper against him. I pull against my restraints, I want to scratch my nails along his skin and grab that hard ass of his. He continues to fuck me hard and my eyes close in delight.

"Open those eyes, sweetheart." Ink growls.

I struggle to obey, but I manage. The pleasure is almost too much for me. My eyes feel heavy with lust. Ink grins; it's a devastatingly handsome smile. "There's those green eyes I love; look at me when you come."

Then he fucks me hard, and I mean hard! I'm screaming, my eyes struggle to remain open but I do it. I scream my release as I look into his dark eyes, all the time he's watching me. His own release quickly follows mine, and he falls on top of me. We're a sweaty mess, but fuck, that was the best sex yet.

Chapter Thirteen

Eve

Elizabeth has gone off to play with Teresa so I can have a shower and get ready for the day. Gabe left early this morning, so I had to ask Teresa to keep an eye on her for me. Elizabeth is a curious child. I know if I let her out of my sight she'll be off exploring the clubhouse alone, which is something I don't want.

The guys here are great and try to keep their bad mouths to themselves as much as they can when she's around, but there are some areas of the clubhouse I've obviously kept her away from.

As I walk out my room, I pass Elvis' old room and pause at the door. I'm filled with sad memories. I wish he was here, so that Elizabeth could meet him. As I'm gathering myself together the door opens, a shocked Sue standing in the doorway. I've seen her around, but we haven't spoken much. I've noticed she's not her usual self, but that's to be expected after the death of Elvis, it's still recent and raw. I feel like there's still something wrong between us. I need to change that.

It's time we have a heart to heat and fix our relationship.

"Hi." I smile; I'm surprised when she smiles back at me.
"Glad to have you back."

I raise my eyebrows. "Really?"

Sue slowly nods her head, indicating the inside of her room. I enter slowly, cautious as the last time I was in here, I was in tears and left with Elvis' blood covered cut.

"Come on in, darling, I'm not going to bite." She smiles. I sit on one of the chairs in the corner and Sue follows. She turns her chair towards me. "Now what do you want to talk about?"

"How are you?"

Her eyes go wide. "Wow, you just jump right in there don't you honey?"

"Oh god, I'm sorry."

She laughs a little, shaking her head. "I'm pulling your leg." She leans back in her chair. "I'm doing ok. No need to worry."

"Really?"

She nods her head. "I'm sorry, Eve."

I know exactly what she's saying sorry for and tears sting my eyes. She's apologizing for blaming me and for what happened in this room right after her old man's death.

"It's ok."

She shakes her head. "No, it's not. What I did was horrible. There was no need for that. Elvis would have spanked my ass for that."
She laughs and I join in.

"I miss him." It slips from my mouth without thinking.

Before I can apologize for what I just said, Sue smiles a sad smile. "Me too, darling. Every second of every day."

I love the way she calls me darling, but at the same time I hate it. It reminds me of Elvis.

Tears gather and I try and hold them back. "He would be pretty damn proud of you, Eve."

I look back up at Sue as she smiles over at me.

"You're a brilliant mother to your girl. I had the pleasure of talking to her yesterday; she's a credit to you."

I can't hold my tears back any more; they fall and drip onto my lap. I quickly try and wipe the rest away. I feel terrible crying in front of Sue.

Sue scoots her chair closer, taking hold of my hand. She begins to tell me a story about Elvis I've never heard. He'd often sit up in the middle of the night, staring out at the night sky in frustration. He'd cry when he spoke of the girl he'd loved and feared he would never see again. How her mother wouldn't let him take her as his own as she grew up. He'd had to watch her being raised in neglect. He wanted to bring her here with him, but her mother wouldn't hear of her leaving and wouldn't let him ask her, so he'd had to leave her behind. I realize the girl is me. My throat becomes tight and I can't speak. Part of me hates my mother right now, but I realize if I hadn't stayed in England I wouldn't have Elizabeth now.

"He loved you like a daughter. I shouldn't have said the things I said. He wanted you here from the moment he returned to this club. He would want you here with Teresa now. I'm just sad he didn't get to meet his granddaughter."

When she calls Elizabeth his granddaughter, my heart fills with love and sadness. I cry, Sue joining in soon after. She holds me tight in her arms.

As we both dry our eyes, there's a knock on the door. Teresa walks in holding Elizabeth's hand. She smiles at seeing us together. "Reminiscing?"

"You bet." Sue replies.

Elizabeth lets go of Teresa's hand, running up to me. She raises her arms. I see she looks tired. It's not time for her mid-day nap quite yet so I sit her on my lap; Sue smiles at her.

"Hello little lady."

"Hi." Elizabeth replies.

"Come on over here and let me tell you all about your grandpa Elvis." Elizabeth scurries down from my knee, excitedly running over to Sue. "Teresa, grab my photo albums from under the bed." Sue requests. Together we spend the next hour talking about Elvis, laughing over the photos Sue has of him until Elizabeth falls asleep and I carry her back to our room.

***

Prez

After sweeping the area, Cowboy and Disney walk back to where Angel and I stand waiting.

"All clear Prez." Disney nods, moving to stand on my left.

"Good." I knew it would be, but with our way of life, you can never be too careful.

The roar of motorcycle engines alerts us to their presence, we stand and wait to meet them in formation. Angel to my right, Cowboy to his right and Disney on my left.

We need to have this meeting, it's been too long coming, but it's taken until now for it to become possible. This shit has gone far enough, it needs to be dealt with. My club brothers, their women and children's lives are at stake right now, that's not making me happy, it's making me extremely pissed off. I've had enough of this shit, so has everyone else involved with the club. My dad didn't pass everything down to me for nothing, there was a fucking reason. I intend to do him proud. I will end this; I am not losing anything more to that shit Satan!

Four men dressed in black stop their bikes right outside the open doors, opposite our bikes, climbing off them slowly and scanning the area. We decided a meeting on neutral ground would be the best idea, we chose this empty warehouse just outside of town. There's no noise, no people, no interruptions. It's perfect.

The deal was that he brought along three of his men and so would I. As I watch Scalp, the president of Carnal MC, get off his bike he's immediately flanked by his men. I glance to my right, making sure Angel is keeping it together. As Satan is a part of their club, Angel naturally hates the whole of Carnal MC. He looks tense and ready to strike at any second. His arms are folded, a scowl in place, he watches the MC make their way over to us. It's only natural that he's pissed off right now, his woman's in danger and so is the little girl he's claimed as his own daughter. Exactly why we need to bring Satan to an end.

I recognize the men Scalp has brought along with him. It's part of my job to know the other MC clubs nearby, and their members. I see Twist, an ugly fucker with long black hair, Scruff who lives up to his name and Sac; I'm not even going to go into the stories I've heard about that one.

Standing face to face, Angel finally speaks. "Where's your VP, Scalp?"

He's taunting Carnal MC's president. I throw him a warning glance that he ignores. We need this meeting to go smoothly and successfully.

Scalp looks to my VP and smirks. "Fuck, it's spooky how you fuckers look exactly alike."

I notice Angels jaw clench, he hates to be reminded who he shares his DNA with, although I doubt he ever could ever forget.

I sigh loudly. "Stop fucking bitching like women, let's get straight down to business."

Scalps dark eyes return to me, he straightens himself up. "Satan is no longer VP of Carnal MC, that honor is now Twists." He inclines his head to his right where Twist stands proudly. Scalp looks back to Angel. Your brother's gone rogue, he's no longer any part of my club. I am tired of the shit he brings to my door, I want nothing to do with him."

I'm surprised and I can see my brothers are as well. We did suspect this might happen, but hearing it has is still a big deal.

"Do you have any idea where he is?" I ask.

"No, but I do know he's back in Australia." Scalp responds.

Before we end the meeting we sort through business that affects both of our clubs. It turns out that Scalp never wanted Satan to be his VP; he'd blackmailed his way up the club and had his eyes set on being the next president. Knowing Satan he wouldn't have waited for the role to come to him naturally, he'd have engineered it sooner rather than later. Everyone was scared of Satan inside the club, even the toughest of men. It's no surprise, if you got on his wrong side he either killed you or you wished he had. Not surprisingly Scalp is glad to finally have him out of his club. Satan brought the club a lot of enemies, Scalp has his work cut out to make everything right again. With his promise that he's no longer an enemy of Severed, we begin to part ways. As the men straddle their bikes, Scalp asks to speak alone with me. Assuring my men that it's fine, I follow Scalp a safe distance where we won't be overheard.

Scalp begins to tell me something I already feared. We have a filthy rat in our club who's been feeding Satan important information. This is a problem we need sorting and Scalp offers to help in any way possible, he's just sorry he doesn't know the rat's identity.

Returning to my precious Harley I ride home, my brothers behind me, I think about my club members and who could do this. Whoever it is, they better pray they keep their lives. We may not be a dangerous and crime filled club, but one rule I do live by is do not betray your brothers.

***

???

Once I've made sure I'm alone, I lock the door. Sliding my phone from my pocket, I look down at it in disgust. With regret rushing through my veins I dial the number I've been given, he answers quickly.

"What do you have for me?"

I take a deep breath. "There was a meeting between Severed and Carnal today. They know you're not part of Carnal anymore, now both clubs are looking for you."

I hear a smash through the phone. "Anything else?!" He screams down the phone.

"Yeah, they know there's a snitch and are looking into it."

He laughs. "Good luck with that."

The line goes dead. I close my eyes, pure hatred for myself rushing through me. Fuck, I need a drink. How the fuck did I ever get pulled into this. I don't want to betray the club, I'd die first, but that fucker Satan has left me with no other choice.

Most of the club don't even know I have a baby sister, I rarely mention her round here, and I sure as fuck never let her visit me here. I know what these guys would want to do to her. She deserves a better life than this. She's beautiful, she's smart and she's destined for better things than hooking up with a biker and this lifestyle.

She's away at college now. I didn't want her to go, but as I'm pretty much persona non grata with my parents due to my lifestyle, I didn't get any say in the matter. She's too far away for me to keep her safe. Of all the threats I imagined for her, this one she's facing never occurred to me, even in my wildest nightmares.

I didn't think anything of the letter postmarked from her college town, even though I didn't recognize the handwriting. I just assumed it was from her. Opening it, a handful of photos fall to the floor, my heart stopping as I recognize the subject in them. It's my baby sister. She's not doing anything wrong in them, just going about her day to day activities. It's the style of the photo that cause my heart to stop. They're surveillance photos. Some fucker is watching her. I quickly scan through them, then come to a piece of paper with just a few lines of type:

I'd hate to see the pretty girl get hurt.
Call me...

There's a mobile number. I'm about to shout for the guys to help me sort this, but some sixth sense stops me. I need to call this fucker and find out what they want first. My first instinct is it's blackmail, they'll be lucky, it's not like I have enough money to pay a ransom demand. I never expected it to be Satan on the other end.

What Satan asks destroys me. He's given me an impossible choice. Either I betray the club, or he'll turn his sick and twisted attention to my baby sister. I'm fucked either way. Even if I agree to this betrayal, I can't guarantee her safety, but if I don't agree, I've signed her death warrant. As hard as the decision is to make, there's really no decision there.

I've tried to give away as little information as possible, Eve's flight time, her address in England, and letting him know she was back. And today's call.

I'd take the cowards way out and kill myself, but even that won't keep my girl safe. I'm damned if I do, and damned if I don't.

Chapter Fourteen

Eve

The following afternoon I'm sitting on a bench, out back of the clubhouse, soaking up the Australian sun with Teresa at my side. We've been watching Elizabeth running around playing with Rabbit and Cherry while we wait for Prez, Gabe, Cowboy and Disney to finish a meeting. It's so funny to watch, two big tattooed bikers running after a squealing little girl, huge smiles plastered on their faces. It looks like they're enjoying it as much as Elizabeth is. It's nice though, it shows that these men are not all scary and tough.

Teresa and I decided to come out here to enjoy the sun as soon as the men left. All they told us was 'it's club business'. I could see from the hard look on Gabe's face that this was important. More than likely it's something to do with Satan. I just want this to be over. I'm fed up of it all, we need to move on, and that means in every aspect, including what happened to me in York, and my injuries. Since we've been back in Severed, it hasn't been like it was when I was last here. Don't get me wrong, being with Gabe is amazing. I know that I love him and he loves me, but we haven't had sex! We've been back almost a week and he hasn't made love to me or even fucked me! I need him to love me, but he won't. I know why, and it makes me hate Satan even more. Gabe is scared to touch me, he's afraid he'll hurt me. My bruises and cuts scare him away, so we haven't had the hot and hard sex that we would usually have. I understand that while we're sharing a room with Elizabeth it's awkward, but there are other rooms in this place! We could sneak off one night for a little bit. Elizabeth had her own room back in England, so she's used to sleeping on her own all night. Gabe hasn't suggested it though, and he's ignored my not so subtle hints and encouragement. I'm left feeling really horny. I'm not usually a sexual person but Gabe has increased my appetite. I clench my legs in frustration. I need some loving.

I hear Teresa giggling quietly. I look over to her and see she's glancing down at my legs. "What's up hon?"

I give her a look; she knows damn well what's wrong. "You know what's wrong."

She tries not to laugh. "Why isn't Angel stepping up to the plate?"

I roll my eyes. "Have you not seen what I look like?"

She waves her hand in the air. "Oh for fucks sake, bloody men. You need to tell him straight, let him know what you need."

Before I can add anything more, I hear loud talking and laughing coming from the men inside the clubhouse. I recognize one voice in particular; hearing Prez's loud laugh lets me know the men are back. Butterflies flutter in my stomach, that means Gabe is back.

I hear the creaking of the door, letting me know that someone is coming outside. I see Elizabeth look up from Rabbits arms where he's caught her. Her eyes light up when she sees who it is, a huge smile spreading across her face. "Angel!" she shrieks.

Rabbit lets her go, keeping an eye on her as she runs over to Angel; we all watch as he pulls her up into his arms, lifting her high. He kisses her on her chubby cheeks. "How's my little princess doing?"

"Wabbit and Chewwy are chasing me." She laughs.

"Did they catch you?"

"Sometimes." She answers.

Prez steps out and Elizabeth spots him over Gabe's shoulder. She reaches out for him so Gabe passes her over to Prez, who bounces her in his large arms, making her giggle. "Uncle Bill." She laughs, spreading kisses all over his face.

He told her not to call him Prez like everyone else; he said she should call him Uncle Bill, because she's special. Now she calls him it with pride. It makes me so happy to see how much she's enjoying her new life here in Severed, and how quickly she's adapted to it.

Now Elizabeth is happily settled with her uncle Bill, Gabe strides over to where I'm sitting, wrapping his arms around me. I lean back into him, sighing happily. I'm relieved he's back and seems to be in one piece. I was secretly scared over what the club business might entail. Gabe kisses me on my forehead, his kisses softly drifting down to my lips, causing goose bumps to break out. His tongue glides along my lips, seeking an invitation, I quickly comply. We both groan as our tongues meet. I grip his leather vest, pulling him closer.

A cough interrupts us and we break apart. I feel like a naughty school girl getting caught behind the bike sheds. Diane stands over us, a knowing grin plastered on her face. "Now I love a good show as much as anyone, but

I'm guessing you don't want your little princess watching her parents getting busy on a bench."

I immediately look around for my daughter. Oh god, what was I thinking? I turn and see she's not where she was the last time I saw her. She was there with Prez just seconds ago! Where has she gone? Before I can freak out, I hear her laugh. She's playing with Rabbit and Cherry again, this time Prez and Teresa have joined in. They're keeping her occupied so she can't see me and Gabe. Watching her play makes me smile.

"Go on you two. Go and disappear."

I look at Diane. I want to but I can't. I begin to shake my head to say no, but Diane places her hands on hips. "Now listen up you two, you've got a family here to help you, and you two need some help right now. We'll watch her while you two see to that itch you need to scratch, don't bother denying it. From the look of that kiss you're seconds away from tearing each other's clothes off and having sex right here! Now get gone and see to your woman, Angel."

I laugh and look across at Gabe, he looks a little unsure. "Angel?"

He looks from Diane and then back to me, seeing my worried look his gaze softens. "I dunno Eve, the doctors-"

"I'm fine." I cut him off. I stand, grabbing hold of his hand to try and pull him up, I can't shift him. He stands anyway, giving me a look of pity at my weakness. He flashes me that panty melting smile of his. "I need you." I whisper in his ear.

His expression goes from smiling to predator in a second. He grips my hand tighter, and turns to Diane. "Keep an eye on our girl for us."

He begins to guide me inside. I can hear Diane laughing as we go. "Don't you worry; take as long as you need."

I follow Gabe into the clubhouse. I know my girl will be perfectly safe with the club members and Diane watching her. They're our family now.

***

I'm naked and Gabe is lying above me, kissing me. He's supporting his weight with his elbows beside my head, trying not to hurt me. I couldn't be happier at this moment. I really need him right now, I need our bond. I need to be connected to Gabe again. He continues to kiss me but it's not enough for me anymore. "Gabe." I plead.

"I don't wanna hurt you, sweetheart."

"You won't. I'm fine." I arch my pelvis towards him, my wetness brushing against his hardness. "Please."

Gabe stares down at me, looking me in the eye as he slowly slides home. My eyes roll back. I groan as he slams into me. It's not as hard as I would like, but yeah, that feels better. When he's fully in, he thrusts again, making sure he's balls deep. It makes me gasp and Gabe growls. "Fuck, I've missed you."

He kisses me as he begins to move again. I want him to move faster and thrust harder, but I know he's trying to be as careful as he can be. Truthfully, I know he needs to be, I'm still sore in places and a little tender from the miscarriage.

No matter how gentle he is, it's still enough to make me moan and cry out loudly, he's finally giving me exactly what I need. I scratch his back, down to his hard ass, digging my nails in as I get closer and closer to my peak.

Ever so gently he reaches down, lifting my waist; just that small movement makes all the difference. His cock hits my sweet spot and I scream out my release. Gabe follows me, growling like a wild animal, but always a gentleman.

***

Elle

After a long flight from London, we've finally arrived at the Severed MC clubhouse Ink has been banging on about ever since I met him. I'm a little surprised; it's a lot nicer than I thought it would be, considering it's a motorcycle club and all. The building itself is large and light colored. A security fence surrounds the perimeter, high and intimidating to look at. A few obviously armed men stand around the courtyard area, guarding the fence I think. It worries me a little that the club needs this much security.

Noticing my wariness, Ink wraps his large tattooed arm around me, pulling me close. I feel safe in his arms. "Don't worry babe, it looks scarier than it really is."

We walk together, Ink's arm still wrapped around my shoulders. There are two men standing guard inside the main gate; as soon as they spot us they let us in. They both sport large friendly smiles when they see Ink.

"You're a sight for sore eyes! Fucking hell man, heard you've been sightseeing?" One of the large men says, slapping his hand on Ink's back.

Ink laughs back. "Yeah man, this pretty lady persuaded me."

Both men look towards me now, taking me in from head to toe. I feel my cheeks blush under their thorough inspection.

The second man steps forward, holding out his hand to me. "Hi gorgeous, I'm Kid."

I smile as I shake his hand. He's a very handsome man, big and very masculine. He's got a shadow of a beard along his strong jaw line, and the brightest green eyes. He's definitely all man, so I've no idea why his nickname is Kid. I know the reason behind Ink, Angel and Cowboy's nicknames so I'm naturally curious.

"Nice to meet you, I'm Elle."

He flashes me a smile I'm sure gets him what he wants with every woman. Not this one though. "Pretty name, for a pretty woman."

"Back off, asshole." Ink pulls me closer, away from Kids' appreciative gaze. I breathe in Inks scent and smile. I like this territorial side of him.

Kid just laughs at Ink and the first man re-joins us after locking the gates. He smiles warmly at me, but instead of a hand shake like Kid, he pulls me in for a hug. "Man, you're beautiful." He pulls me back, giving me a cheeky wink. "The names Ice."

Ink yanks me back from Ice's grip, shooting him a glare. "Hands off, fuckers. You know she just fucking walked in with me."

I stand back from Inks hold. I may like a little bit of jealousy, but that was taking it too far for my liking. "She has a name Ink; I'm not some property you can piss all over!"
I cross my arms over my chest to prove my point, causing Ice to immediately look down at my boobs; I don't really care right now. Kid looks like he's holding in his laugh, but he's not doing a great job of it. "Man, she's sure gonna fit in well around here."

Ink shoves his hand through his hair, sighing. "I didn't mean it like that, babe."

I look away from him because I'm pissed. "Take me to Eve, now."

He tries to take hold of my hand but I move it away in time. I don't want to act all friendly right now. I want to talk to my friend. I hear a heavy sigh, and then Ink walks in front as he guides me inside. I'm so eager to see Eve!

***

After gossiping about my travels with Eve and her friends, Diane and Teresa, we move outside to the outdoor area where the men are preparing a barbecue. It smells amazing. I try not to look around too much because I know Ink is out here and I feel a little silly. When I first saw Eve and the girls, Eve jumped straight in, asking me what was wrong. After Ink left us to it, I filled them in on what he'd said outside. The women giggled at me, telling me that's how these men act. They think they're the shit around here, acting all alpha around each other, especially when it comes to women. Apparently, what Ink had said was the norm around here, nothing to kick up a fuss about. Now I feel stupid for over reacting.

Everywhere I look there are men dressed in black and leather, most of them sporting tattoos and beards'. This is a girl's wet dream, a darkest fantasy come true, especially mine. One of mine includes a dark, dangerous biker taking me hard and fast, totally ignoring my needs. To be used as his play thing, for his pleasure alone. Just thinking about it warms me from the inside; I clench my thighs in need.

After laughing with the women for a while, a little body runs right into me. I look down to see adorable little Elizabeth smiling up at me. "Hi, Elle!"

"Hey there princess, how do you like your new home?"

Her eyes sparkle. "I love it!"

To prove to me that she really does love it here, she runs off without another word and jumps right up at Cowboy who happily throws her in the air. Her laughter fills the space; I smile at how happy she looks. Eve and Elizabeth have found a family here. I'm jealous.

Teresa sits beside me, handing me a much needed beer. "How are you liking Severed?"

I smile at her; I'm aware of her and Eve's friendship and know about their recent struggles. Watching them today I can see they're working it out. Everyone here has been nice and welcoming, well apart from the skanky looking girls who wander around. I've noticed they've been shooting me daggers. Eve told me they're the club whores. They don't look trashy enough to not be allowed around the children, but they reek of desperation. The way they look at the bikers, you can tell they've only one thing on their minds. Apart from them, everyone else has been friendly enough. Nothing at all like the bitches I knew growing up.

***

When the sky has darkened, the drinks are pouring, and the food has all been eaten, Eve puts a tired Elizabeth to bed. When she returns she sighs happily. "Fast asleep."

"How are you feeling about having to stay here?"

Her smiles drops and she shrugs her shoulders. "It's not the best situation, but me and my girl are safe here, that's all that matters. Until Satan is dealt with, we have no choice but to stay here."

I know perfectly well how Satan will be dealt with. After hearing everything he's put these people through, I can't agree more. I hope I never get to meet the man, from the stories I've heard, I have a feeling I wouldn't live to tell the tale.

I feel someone sit down beside me, and recognize Ice smiling at me. He really is a good looking man, gorgeous smile, deep dimples and dark blue eyes. He's got tattoos all along his arms, but he's a bit too much of a beef cake for me. He's a huge man, muscles aside, he's sexy as hell.

"Hey gorgeous, nice to see you again."

"Hi, Ice."

"You two already met?" Eve asks.

"Yeah, out front when she got out of the cab with Ink." Ice answers her.

He smiles over at Eve; I see the respect shining out of his eyes. He's a good man I can tell. Very mischievous though.

"So where is your boyfriend, Elle?"
I shake my head. "He's not my boyfriend."

He quirks an eyebrow. "Sure seems that way from the look he's shooting me."

I look over my shoulder, sure enough, there's a very pissed off looking Ink glaring over at us.

I feel Ice scoot closer to me. I take my eyes off Ink, downing a big gulp of beer. "Elle, you can do better than Ink. You seem like a nice girl. Ink doesn't stay around much."

I look over at him. "Don't worry, I'm a big girl."

He gives me a genuine smile. I need to change the subject. Shit is getting serious.

"So, the person I can do better with, wouldn't happen to be you now would it?"

He grins cheekily. "If you think so."

I laugh loudly. "What's the story behind your name anyway?"

He grins wide. "I like ice." He simply answers.

I narrow my eyes at him. "That's it? You just like ice?"

Eve giggles beside me and Angel sits down beside her. "It what he loves doing with the ice, Elle."

Eve giggles again; Angel has a sly smirk on his face. I look back to Ice and he wiggles his eyebrows. "Wanna find out just how much?"
My mouth drops open in shock, before I can answer Ink stands in front of me, pulling me up. I slam into his hard body. When I look up at him he's glaring at Ice. Ice just smiles right back. "Keep your ice away from her pussy, you fucker!"

Before I can react to what he's just said Ink leads me away. I'm left completely speechless. I'm all for the kink, but ice? Down there? Wow!

I start to think about it, images appearing in my mind. My body warms again from my earlier fantasies.

***

Ink

I don't know why I'm so pissed off, but I am!

Elle isn't my woman, but I didn't like watching all my brothers drooling over her, then Ice had to go over there and fucking flirt with her right in my face. Minutes earlier he'd been standing with me, joking about me staring at her, and telling me to go over to her. But I didn't. Instead he went over and made her giggle and laugh. When I heard him explaining his biker name to her, I saw red.

I don't know what's fucking wrong with me!

Elle is a beautiful woman, and we've had a great time together. It's just sex. That's all it was ever supposed to be, so why did I react the way that I did?

I storm my way through the clubhouse, not giving a shit. They all move out of my way. I need to get Elle to my room right now. I need to be buried deep inside her. I want her to forget about every other man, and just focus on me. She can't be mine forever, but she can be mine right now.

I push open my door, pulling Elle in after me, before kicking it shut. I place my hand on Elle's chest, pushing her back against the wall. Resting my arms either side of her face, I breathe her scent in to calm me down. Her eyes are wide as I lean in to claim her plump lips. She moans against my mouth and I marvel at the sound.

"Naked." I manage to order, in between our kissing.

She unbuttons her blouse, her fingers moving too slow for my liking. Growing impatient I move her hands away, yanking open her top, buttons fly everywhere, hitting everything. She gasps, but I have no time to waste. I quickly unbutton her jeans and order her to pull them down while I get naked myself.

I take in her delicate beauty as she stands before me, waiting for me to make a move. She deserves pleasure and I'm more than happy to supply it. For some reason, I feel like I need to do this for her, and nobody else should. The thought of any other man making Elle climax, seeing her eyes rolling back and her mouth part, it makes me pissed to think of someone else seeing her like that.

With that thought I pull hard on her hair, revealing her neck. I lick from her collar bone to her ear lobe. I grab her ass with my other hand, pulling her close. Her softness against my hard dick. Because I've already covered myself with a condom I don't think twice about pushing straight into her pussy. I growl, a glorious feeling overtaking me, my animal instinct rules me and I pound harder. Fucking her against the wall. Elle's eyes roll back, her mouth drops open. That look is so fucking hot, I'm glad I'm the one to put it there. I fuck her harder, needing her to know exactly who's giving this to her.

"Oh god, Ink!"

Yeah, that's exactly what I'm talking about! I slam harder, pulling her hair and making her scream. Her nails claw at me, which only spurs me on more.

I lift her up, supporting her weight with my hands on her perfect ass. I walk us to the bed, still inside her. I throw her down, making her giggle. She smiles up at me, her smile making me pause for a second. Snapping myself out of it, I crawl on top of her. Taking in her glorious body as I go, I lick my way up from her belly button. I bite down on her hard nipples, and slam back into her wet and ready pussy. Her walls clamp around me and she moans loudly. I continue to fuck her as she climaxes around me. It's not long until I follow her. I look down at her smiling, satisfied face.

"Wow." She whispers up at me, looking a little tired all of a sudden.

"Yeah, you can say that babe."

I go to the bathroom clean myself up, and then I join Elle back in bed.

Chapter Fifteen

Elle

Waking up the next morning, I feel tired and satisfied. I stretch out, expecting to bump into the man beside me, but I don't feel a warm naked body at all.

I roll over and see the space next to me is empty. He's probably in the bathroom. I reach for my phone to check the time. It's just past 7am so instead of falling back to sleep, I start to play Candy Crush to pass the time. It's become my latest addiction.

When ten minutes have passed I start to wonder where he is, but still wait.

When twenty minutes pass, I put down my phone and sit up. I was going to give him a bit of morning action, but I'm growing impatient.

I get out of bed, gloriously naked, walking over to the small bathroom in the corner.

"Ink?" I wait, there's no answer. I knock on the bathroom door. "Ink?"

Again, no answer. I slowly open the door, popping my head around, it's empty. I spin around, suddenly flooded with disappointment. He left me in bed! Ink never gets up before 10 am! He's not a morning person at all!

That means one thing, he didn't sleep with me last night. But why?

We slept in the same bed while we were in Edinburgh, Newcastle and London but now we've come back to his home, he's left me in the bed alone! I know he was in the bed during the night, I woke and cuddled up to him, so what happened?

Teresa put my bags away when I arrived yesterday and I've yet to ask her where she put them. I look around at my discarded clothes on the floor. My jeans are tossed in a heap, and my blouse is ripped, fucking hell I loved that blouse!

Well I'm not waiting for Ink any longer. Seeing as it's early I don't think a load of bikers will be up yet. I really don't want to put on my tight jeans from yesterday, so I look through the wardrobe in Ink's room.

I open the drawer along the bottom first and almost laugh. Why would a man need so many black jeans?

Opening the wardrobe, I see a long line of white shirts and black shirts. Wow, Ink loves color!

I grab one of the black shirts, putting it on, not even bothering with a bra. I'm a woman on a mission. I need to find Ink.

Opening the door, I look left and right, I can't see anyone so far. Slowly I creep down the hallway, coming to the main area. It's empty, as I thought it would be.
I hear a noise from the other side of the door from the bar room. I quietly begin to walk over, wondering who it could be.

When I approach the door I notice it's slightly open, enough for me to take a peek. What I see shocks the fucking shit out of me! I've seen a lot of things in my life, especially on my travels but not something like this. I don't know whether to go away while I can, or continue watching.

On one of the large square tables in the middle of the bar lies Diane, she is completely naked. She's blindfolded, gagged and tied to the corners. Above her stands Dragon, her old man I met yesterday. He has this long, thin feather whip and is drifting it up and down her body. I can see Diane breathing heavily, when Dragon glides it in between her thighs she groans.

Dragon suddenly drops the feather whip to kneel between her spread thighs. I hear Diane gasp and see her back arch. Dragon growls like a mad man as he digs his face in deeper, making Diane moan louder. I'm rooted to the spot, I can't move! What if I get caught watching?

I feel a body come up behind me, a hand comes over my mouth. "What are you up to, babe?"

I relax into Ink's body, forgetting that I'm supposed to be angry at him. His stubble scratches the back of my neck. "They love to have sex anywhere they can, hoping that they'll get caught or that someone watches from the shadows."

Oh my god, is he telling me the truth? Diane and Dragon get off on this? They want to be watched?

I look at Diane, totally on display, thinking to myself that if someone saw me like that I'd be mortified!
Dragon reaches down and picks up a long thin object. He raises it high before smacking it down on Diane's quivering body. If Ink's hand hadn't been over my mouth I'd have gasped out loud, alerting them that I was watching!

I continue to watch as Dragon whips her again and again, muttering dirty words to her the whole time. Ink begins to kiss the back of my neck, shivers travelling along my spine. He bites my ear lobe, and my head falls back onto his shoulder. His hand goes to my thigh, slowly travelling up under the loose shirt I'm wearing. My breathing starts to match Diane's, Ink's fingers brush my folds.

"Watch them." He whispers in my ear.

I lift my head back up, opening my eyes. Dragon is now fucking Diane with no mercy, smacking her thighs as he does. Ink's finger dips inside my wet pussy and my legs buckle. Watching the scene in front of me, and having Ink play with me has me turned on so much I almost feel the need to beg for a release. I forget that I'm angry at him and that somebody could be watching us, like we're watching Diane and Dragon.

As Dragon whips and fucks Diane harder, Ink spins me around and lifts me. Quickly carrying me to the bedroom where he fucks me so hard, I climax three times before he collapses at the side of me.

I fucking love make up sex.

***

Eve

After a much needed catch up with Elle about her and Ink, we finally decide to surface from my room. We need some fresh air, and sun on our skin. We're wearing big, silly grins as we walk into the main area of the clubhouse. Our chat was packed full of giggles and lots of graphic details. Elle wouldn't give me any unless I gave her something in return, so we swapped stories and gossip about our men until we had our fill. I can't believe Elle didn't tell me about Inks pierced cock sooner! I mean, how can you keep that a secret?

I look around, searching for Gabe, but I can't see him. I do however spot Elizabeth sitting at a table with Rabbit and Kid. When I approach them I can see that they're coloring in pretty pictures of butterflies and flowers. I laugh as I sit down beside Elizabeth giving her a kiss. "Hey baby, having fun?"

She nods her head enthusiastically, continues her coloring. Her tongue darting out to the side as she concentrates. I look at the guys. "Where's Angel?"

Kid looks up from his important task of coloring. "Out with Prez. Ice said there was a meeting. Looked important."

I cock my head to the side. "So why aren't you there?"

He smirks. "Club business sweetheart."

I huff, leaning down closer to Elizabeth. "Wanna go play outside?"

She slams her crayons down, shouting, "Yeah!"

Rabbit stops what he's doing. "You won't wanna take her outside, Eve."

"Why not?" Elle asks.

"Because it's best for Elizabeth that she not see what's out there." He snickers.

This spikes my curiosity, by the look on Elle's face, hers as well.

"We can go out though, right?" I ask. They both nod, they look like they're trying to hold in their laughter and I narrow my eyes.

"Sure." Kid answers.

"Watch her for me." I tell them as I kiss Elizabeth's head. They both nod, continuing with their coloring. "Be back in a minute baby."

As Elle and I make our way to the bar that leads out to the back, I can hear their snickering. Elle and I share a confused look, but carry on walking. When we step outside we frown at each other, there's nobody out here and I can't see anything that would keep them from letting Elizabeth outside. Shrugging our shoulders, we walk over to our favorite bench that always catches the sun.

That's when we spot him. The reason why Kid and Rabbit wouldn't bring my sweet, innocent baby girl out here. I'm so relieved that they didn't.

A gloriously naked man is reclining in a deck chair in the late afternoon sun, only a hand protecting his modesty. He's around the corner from the doorway, so that's why we didn't see him straight away, but now we see all of him. And I mean ALL of him. His eyes are closed. His skin is tanned a golden color and covered in some large, tribal tattoos. His body is in great shape, ripped muscles and hard abs.

Elle and I stand and stare.

"Holy hell" Elle gasps, "who's the hottie?"

"Oh my fucking god." I whisper to Elle.

"I've died and gone to biker heaven." She whispers back.

I can't help but laugh; then freeze when I realize the naked man has heard me. He slowly raises his head, flashing us a smile. "Hello there, ladies."

He sits up and because we're standing to the side of him, we can't quite see his private area. He doesn't seem at all bothered about his nakedness as he talks to us. "Had to top up the tan."

As if that's the most normal explanation. God I'm glad the guys didn't bring out Elizabeth.

"Who are you?" I finally manage to ask.

He quickly stands, flashing us his marvelous ass and shrugs on his black jeans. When he's partially decent, he walks over to us.

"I'm Justice." He holds out his hand to Elle. I see her struggle to move her eyes from his toned chest.

"Elle." She responds.

He holds out his hand to me, and now he's fully facing me. I take a quick peek at his chest before accepting his handshake. "Eve."

He places his hands into his pockets, smiles a great big charming smile. If I wasn't so in love with my Gabe, I'd be a pool on the floor right now.

"Nice to meet you beautiful ladies."

Suddenly there's a loud bang. I don't turn to find out what it is, or shall I say who it is. I see Justice tense as he watches over my shoulder. Then the voice I adore turns into a very loud roar as he shouts across the yard.

"Step away from my old lady, Justice!"

Justice holds out his arms wide, a look of innocence on his face. "Which one of these beautiful ladies is yours?"

I give him a small, slight wave. "That would be me."

Justice lands his eyes back on me, slowly taking me in, before nodding his head. In that moment Gabe storms over, I can hear his boots hitting the ground as he does. When he reaches me, he pulls me close, glaring across at Justice. Gabe is a well built and tall man and Justice evenly matches him.

"Nice to see you again, Angel." He nods his head in respect to Gabe.

Out of the corner of my eye, I notice that Ink steps closer to Elle. Justice sees this as well, flashing a smile at Elle to taunt Ink. As soon as he does, Ink shoves Elle behind him; in the same stance Gabe has placed himself in, in front of me. I'm surprised to see Elle just roll her eyes in response. Usually she would shout at Ink or come back with some witty remark. If I didn't know better, I'd think that she's enjoying this side of Ink now.

Justice shakes his head in mock disappointment. "Seems all the best women around here are taken."

"Damn straight." Prez says from behind us. I notice Justice stand straighter when he hears Prez, before turning around to see Prez has his arm around Teresa who's giggling.

"Prez." Justice nods, Prez smiles back with a head nod of his own.

Just then I see Elizabeth appear, running out of the clubhouse, a guilty looking Kid and Rabbit following closely behind her. I look around and see that almost every biker is out here watching everything unfold. It's probably why Elizabeth has come out, thinking that she's missing something. I shake my head at the sight of them all watching. Nosey ass bikers.

Elizabeth wedges herself in between Gabe and I. Justice looks down, surprised by her appearance. He smiles down at her. "Well who's this pretty little lady?"

She swings her dress from side to side. "Lizabeth." She drawls shyly.

Justice bends down to her level. "That's a very nice name you have."

Elizabeth giggles. Gabe reaches down to pick her up. Justice stands again and looks from Gabe who's holding Elizabeth, then to me. "Well no wonder you're such a pretty girl, you have a beautiful momma."

My, my, this man is a charmer. Gabe's scowl deepens and Justice laughs at his expression.

"Chill out, Angel. I'm messing with ya. Besides, why didn't you tell me you finally got yourself an old lady and had a baby?"

Justice ruffles Elizabeth's curls. Ink steps forward. "Prez, who the fuck is this?"

Gabe snaps his head toward Ink "Language!"

"Shit I'm sorry." Ink slaps his head. "Sorry!"

Some of the guys laugh and I can't help smiling. Ink flashes me a guilty look. I shake my head to let him know it's fine. He didn't mean to do it.

Prez releases Teresa and steps beside Justice. He looks out at everyone and smacks a hand down on Justice's shoulder. "This here is my nephew, Justice. He wants to join us here in Severed; he's come over from the Adelaide charter."

I'm shocked. I didn't know he had a nephew!

Prez pats him on the back before giving him that man hug they all seem to do around here. "It's good to have you home."

"It's good to be back." Justice replies then works his way around the group, introducing himself.

When he gets to Gabe they look at each other for a couple of minutes in silence until Justice breaks out into a smile and Gabe smiles back. Thank goodness!

"It's good to see you." Gabe says as they awkwardly do the back slap while Gabe holds onto Elizabeth.

Justice nods. "Yeah, I missed this place."

They go into a full blown talk down memory lane. It seems Gabe and Justice know each other well. With Gabe and Prez growing up together, and then becoming VP of Severed, he saw a lot of Justice. Justice grew up around the club and was actually a prospect here before Prez became president of the club, he moved to another charter. Part of the reason I'm shocked that Prez has a nephew as old as Justice is because Prez himself doesn't look that old; not that Justice is old. He looks to be around twenty two, Prez only looking a few years older than him. Gabe later tells me that

Prez is the youngest out of all his siblings, so he's a young uncle. That's why he and Justice are so close in age.

I look around at the sight of everyone welcoming our newest member. Gabe told me the club still has to vote him in during a church meeting, but seeing how warmly he's being welcomed and as he's the president's nephew, I'm pretty sure that'll just be a formality.

I laugh as the club whores rush over to the new sexy member, and the sight of the other bikers keeping their old ladies a safe distance away from him.

Justice turns toward where I'm sitting with Gabe, Ink and Elle, he raises his beer in a salute. I just know things will get interesting with Justice around.

***

Eve

Noticing that Elizabeth eyes look a little heavy I decide she she's ready for her bed. Actually, her bedtime was half an hour ago but she begged me for more time, running over and sitting on Cowboy's knee in the main TV area. I don't know how she did it but she somehow persuaded a room full of bikers to watch cartoons, and she cuddled up with Cowboy for all of her extra half an hour..

Now though, she's looking really tired. When I approach her, instead of arguing this time, she lifts her arms for me to pick her up. I carry her to our room, and as I lay her down Gabe enters, a happy smile on his face. It's good to see him smiling. He's been so tense lately. I know it's to do with whatever he's got planned for Satan. I've been secretly worried about him, so it's good to see him looking carefree and happy. There's just something about his smile that makes me fall a little deeper for him every time I see it.

"Hi, sweetheart." He greets me with a kiss." Is it Princess's bedtime?" He looks down at Elizabeth in her cot bed, but as soon as she heard him walk in the room she hid under her bed cover. We can hear her laughing. Gabe acts as though he doesn't know where she is. "Oh no, where's she gone?" Another giggle comes from Elizabeth. Gabe looks around the room. "Is she behind the door?" Elizabeth giggles some more. The whole exchange is making me smile. Gabe is so good to her.

Gabe flashes me a smile as he rips the quilt from on top of her, revealing a laughing Elizabeth, who's kicking her legs in the air.

"Were you hiding?"

Elizabeth giggles as she bobs her head up and down. "Yes daddy."

My heart stops beating as Gabe turns to look at me. His eyes are wide. I shrug my shoulders but he still stares at me. I'm worried he's going to start freaking out on me.

I walk over to Elizabeth who lets out a massive, but very cute yawn. "Elizabeth, why did you call Angel your daddy?"

"'Cause he's my daddy." She says simply.

I turn to Gabe, now instead of the frozen scared look on his face; he has his smile back in place.

"You ok with that?" I ask him.

He dips, kissing Elizabeth on her forehead, and then turns to me. He wraps his tattooed arms around me, and delivers a heart melting kiss. "Fucking ecstatic, sweetheart." He mumbles into my ear.
God this man makes me so happy.

I walk to the toy tidy that Gabe built for Elizabeth's numerous toys and grab some books for her to choose from. Gabe takes them out of my hands. "I've got this."

"Ok." I grin, a huge and stupidly goofy grin, watching as he walks back to Elizabeth's bed.

He turns to me. "I can do this, sweetheart; you go and relax while I put our little princess to sleep."

"Little pwincess." Elizabeth repeats, laughing and I leave them to it.
I don't leave completely though. I stand just out the door to listen in.

"Right, gorgeous. Which book are we reading tonight?"

"Pwincess one." She demands and I smile.

I overhear Gabe laugh. "Erm, no Elizabeth. I don't think princess stories are my thing."

"Daddy don't like pwincesse's?"

"No baby, daddy doesn't like princess stories, but I love you and mummy, you're my princesses."

Tears form in my eyes.

"How about the Gruffallo?" Gabe asks. Elizabeth must have nodded her head because Gabe starts to read.

It's so fucking adorable! Gabe makes all the right noises and uses different voices and Elizabeth gasps and giggles in all the right places. Happy tears fall as I listen in.

When he's finished with the story I hear him kiss her again and he whispers, "night, night princess."

"Night, night, daddy." She answers. I know from experience she will roll onto her side now and snuggle herself to sleep with her bear.

I'm not quick enough to scamper away before Gabe leaves the room, so when we walks out and quietly shuts the door, he catches me.

"Enjoy the story?" He teases me, pulling me into a tight embrace.

All I can manage is a sniffle and a smile.

"What's wrong?" He looks at me with concern.

"Absolutely nothing."

"She called me Daddy." He beams proudly, and I laugh.

"Yeah, she did."

"I love you." He looks at me, suddenly serious.

"I love you too." His lips are quick to kiss mine, and I moan against him. Before I can fully appreciate it though, he's moved away... "This is what I want. You and that beautiful girl in there."

"I want it too." I whisper back.

"No, listen to me. I really want it. I'll make it safe. Nobody will ever hurt you again. You'll be mine forever, wearing my ring and giving birth to my babies."

My heart fills with love for this man. What did I ever do to deserve this kind of love in my life?

"Once this is all done and dusted, we're getting a house. The whole family shit. Big garden, a white fence, swings, slides and toys covering the grass. I love you."

I don't let him say anymore. I reach up and grab his face. I need his lips on mine. It starts to get a little heated and I gasp when I hear someone clear their throat. I turn to see Disney standing there, a huge smile on his face.

"My rooms free." Is all he says, before tossing a set of keys to Gabe and walking off.

Gabe doesn't say anything as he pulls me along, stopping outside a door I'm assuming is Disney's room and unlocking it. As soon as we get in, Gabe locks it then pushes me up against the wall, stripping me of my clothing.

Let's just say, Gabe isn't gentle with me at all.

I have my biker back.

Chapter Sixteen

Elle

I walk out of the room I've been sharing with Ink since we got here. Dressed in shorts and a plain vest, I'm ready to meet Eve.

I'm in a particularly good mood today, odd since I've not enjoyed being kept inside this place all day, every day. How can I not be in a good mood though when Ink keeps me so well entertained?

These past few weeks have been crazy! Literally every day since the hotel in York, we have had sex. It's as though when we're together we just can't seem to get enough of each other. Well, that's how it feels for me anyway.

After giving me a good morning wake up session, Ink had to leave for work at his tattoo shop. I was pleased to get a text message from Eve first thing. She wants me to meet her out back for a catch up. I'm guessing it's going to be more of a bitch fest, but whatever. I need something to keep me busy until Ink returns. I'm already thinking of surprising him with some more sexy lingerie when he gets back.

I open the door, breathing in the fresh morning air and spot Eve on a bench. She's watching Elizabeth ride along on the bike Angel bought her yesterday. The poor girl is getting bored being stuck in this place. The only area us girls are now allowed outside in is this tiny area of garden and play park. Prez thinks this is the only space where the guys can keep us safe.

I almost laugh watching her scowl at the members casually standing around, acting like they want to be outside. More likely they are here standing guard. Poor Eve can't go to the bathroom without having someone on her tail if Angel's not here.

***

Ink

My heads pretty fucked up right now. I have no fucking clue why!

I should be happy. I should be buried deep in Elle's pussy right now, but I feel like I need a little distance. Something's happening between us, I can feel it. I don't know what it is, but it's freaking me the fuck out!

I'm glad to be working in my shop in Severed today. Not only is this whole thing with me and Elle confusing me, but I needed to get out of the clubhouse. I love that place, it's my home but I don't want to be there every minute of every day.

I set up my work space in the room in the back, ready for my next appointment.

***

Twenty minutes later a blonde bombshell strides in wearing a small red dress, my dick stands to attention.
Shit. I don't know what to do. Do I be me? Flirt like shit with her to get what I always want, or do nothing at all? I should act like a man because I have Elle waiting for me back at the clubhouse. I picture Elle's gorgeous face,

her plump pink lips and bright green eyes, her large breasts and golden hair.

"Hi, I have an appointment." She walks right up to the girl sat at reception. She's a club member's daughter. Everyone who works here is connected in some way to Severed MC. It's the way I like it.

She's shown in my direction as I lean against the door frame and smile. I see her eyes widen a little as she takes me in then starts to walk over. I lead her into my room, shutting the door behind us. She waits for me to tell her where to sit and we get started.

"So what can I do for you today?" I ask her.

"I want a tattoo." She quickly answers. Her voice is cultured and there's an air about her. She may look hot but she's no club whore that's for sure. She's almost as classy as Elle, but not quite. There's something about her that reminds me of Elle though, not that I can put my finger on it.

"You're in the right place for that babe."

She blushes a little, tucking her hair behind her ear. "I've already got a scarab beetle on my back that symbolizes protection and good luck; it's in my birthstone colors. I had it done before my first lot of chemo; I wanted something to keep me safe."

This sparks my interest. Not many women ask for a tattoo that means protection. Good luck, yes but protection is a little different. And she mentioned chemo. Looks like, as young as she is she's had a hard time of it.

"You have anything in mind?" I ask.

"Well I chose the scarab beetle because I'm into Egyptology, but I'd like to go for a Chinese dragon this time, for the symbolism. I want to show the strength I've got now I've beaten the cancer." Wow. She has been through some shit. I move over to the shelf, fetching down a folder with pictures and sketches that relate to what she's asking for.

I nod my head in thought as I search for the image I know would be perfect for her. I show her the sketch and her face breaks out in a huge smile. "That's perfect." It's a dragon that covers the whole of her shoulder, and instead of breathing fire, it's breathing life into some trees and bushes. It's an oriental design.

I flash her my smile. "I do my best to please."

At my words she blushes again, and my body responds. Shit. I need to get it together.

Because the piece is going on the back of her shoulder she sits on the table facing away from me. Her body is warm as I touch it and she breaks out in goose bumps. I know she's affected by me because her breathing deepens. She leans into my touch where my hand brushes her skin. Shit, the woman has me hard!

"So what's your name again?" I ask her as I continue with her stencil. I need to break this sexual vibe.

"Emma. What's yours?"

"Ink."

She laughs. "Fitting."

When the transfer for the tattoo is complete I show her it in the mirror. She seems really happy with how it looks. I'm not surprised, my customers are always happy when they leave here. She's so happy that she jumps in my arms, hugging me.

"Thanks, Ink. That's going to be perfect."

I look down at her in my arms, my cock jumping to attention. She feels it against her flat stomach, biting down on her bottom lip.

"You know, I could thank you for it."

"What do you mean babe?"

She trails a finger down my tattooed arm. "How about I let you use me however you want. Right here. No strings?"

Fuck!

My grip on her loosens. I take a step back. "I dunno, babe."

She steps closer. "Come on Ink. Just a little fun. You can do the tattoo when we're done. I promise I won't be all clingy afterwards. It's just sex for the fun of it."

She gets down on her knees, reaching for my belt. I grab onto her hand, stopping her movements. She looks up at me in confusion. She's sexy as hell. "No strings. Just some fun, then I'm gone."

I don't let myself think anymore. I let her hand go, and she gets to work. My head falls back as she takes me in her mouth. Her tongue works wonders on my tip, working around my piercings. She moans as she bites on them. "I love these."

When I've had enough I pull her up, take out a condom from my pocket and sheathe myself. I bend Emma forward over the table where she was just sitting, sliding right in to her ready pussy from behind. We both groan loudly. I pump harder, trying to find my release. The metal table starts to make squeaking noises under us, so I lift her and walk us over to the nearest wall. I push her back against the cold wall, slide right back inside and fuck her harder, and harder. We're both still fully clothed, me in my shirt with my jeans pulled down below my ass and Emma still with her dress held up around her bust and now up around her waist, her skimpy knickers pulled to the side.

Her legs tighten their grip around me as her climax nears. I feel mine coming on too. I take a tighter hold of her waist as I bury myself balls deep, letting my piercing hit her magic spot until she comes, her walls clamping around me. Milking me for all I've got.

She smiles as I withdraw my now drained cock, putting her underwear back in place.

"That was great!" She licks her lips in satisfaction. "Hard and fast, just how I like it." She smirks at me. "Now let's get on with this tattoo!"

I can't believe I just did that. I feel like I've betrayed Elle, yet neither of us ever made a commitment or any promises to each other. Yes, the sex was great, but it missed the spark of that something extra when I'm with Elle. I'm going to have to come clean with her. For the next few hours while I concentrate on Emma's tattoo my mind is torn. Do I tell Elle or do I just forget about it.

Emma is an ideal client; she's handling the pain really well. I think she senses my guilt though as at one point she looks back at me. "Ink, it's okay. It was a one off, an itch I needed to scratch. I'm not going to try and come between you and whoever you're stressing over right now." She gives me a gentle smile. This chick is a class act.

When it's finished the dragon looks great on Emma's back, she's delighted with the end result. I book a follow up appointment to add some elements of color for her in a few weeks when it's settled. I'm such a pussy I actually consider switching her over to one of the other guys for that appointment.

I'm done for the day and shut up shop, everyone else has already gone. As I climb on my bike I wonder how the hell I'm going to tell Elle I just fucked up - big time.

Chapter Seventeen

Satan

Severed MC has to be the most boring fucking MC in the history of MC's. I've been watching the compound for a few days now and nothing happens. I'm guessing they're on lockdown; I haven't seen any of the whores going in and out, come to think of it I haven't seen any bitches at all yet. All I've seen is these ugly fuckers ride in and out on their pussy excuses for bikes.

My little rat is running scared; perhaps I'll have to pay a visit to baby sister to give them an incentive to give me some decent fucking information. I already know Angel has Eve tucked away safely in the clubhouse, I need to know when she's stepping foot outside so I can get hold of her. Lockdown doesn't seem to stop these Severed bitches having their little jaunts, it can't be too much longer now before they go stir crazy and head on out. I'll be ready for them when they do.

I pull my blade from my boot, and start to sharpen it while I watch the back yard of the compound. The action calms me, the monotonous swipe of the sharpener as it hones the blade. It's a sweet sound, not quite as sweet as Eve's whimper will be as I draw the tip of the blade against her throat though. Just thinking about Eve begging for her life has me hard. I like using my knife on bitches, teasing them as I cut oh so gently into their flesh, barely scratching the surface, just enough for droplets of blood to appear. For me that's foreplay. Nothing gets me as hard as drawing my blade against the skin of a naked woman. Holding the knife against their pretty little neck as I thrust into them from behind. I don't want to see their face, I never want to see their faces - but I'll make an exception for Eve.

When I've come, deep inside of them, I flip them over, carving my mark into their belly. I mark my property, even if I'm only going to take it that one time. If they've pleased me, they'll live to see another day, if they haven't, well then I fuck them with my knife. I watch the blood draining out of them, mixing with my semen. Then, like the used trash they are, I get a prospect to dispose of them. I want more than that with Eve. I want to take Eve every way possible, I want to mark each inch of that white skin with my brand. I want to fuck her till she pleads for me to kill her, but most of all, I want to hear her scream for Angel while I do it and have the fucker watch!

Just thinking about what I want to do has my cock straining so hard against my jeans, it's almost painful. I reach down and release my cock, tracing the blunt edge of the blade slowly up and down my throbbing erection. That excites me even more. I fist my cock, fucking my hand, it's Eve's defeated, tear stained face I see as I spurt my release all over the ground in front of me. If just thinking about what I'm going to do to her gives me an orgasm I can't wait to see how it feels when it's for real!

There's movement in the back of the compound. There's a child running towards the swings, a couple of biker's following behind, scanning the area. They're armed; I can see the holsters under their cuts. Stupid fuckers, I could take one of them out from here with my knife, I'm so close and they've no idea I'm here.

I turn my attention to the child. It's Eve's brat. Torturing her would be sweet, especially if mummy was watching. I'll settle for killing Eve for now, if I get the brat as well, it's a bonus.

That said, if I don't take the brat now, it will be all the sweeter later when I do come back for her. I can wait. Contrary to belief, I'm a patient man. I'll bide my time and wait until she's older, old enough for me to be her first...

And her last.

I can wait long enough for Angel to have grown attached to her. I get to hurt the bastard twice that way.

I turn my attention back to my blade, resuming the sharpening. I can't hear what's being said down there, just the murmur of voices and the high pitched sound of the brat's laughter. I can wait. Sometime Eve is going to leave that compound, and when she does, she'll be running straight into my arms.

***

Angel

Elizabeth is bored of playing indoors. She can see the swing set and the sandpit from the window. We had it built for the members kids when we have our get-togethers. Elizabeth's looking at them with such longing I give in. We've got guards stationed around the compound and the play area is close to the clubhouse. I call Disney and Ice over to help me keep an eye on her. Cowboy's Elizabeth's favorite but he's off running errands for Prez right now, and Ink is working.

"Princess." I call over to her. She instantly recognizes my pet name for her and turns to me, her beaming smile warming my heart. This little girl has really taken to me, and I've fallen head over heels for her, that's for sure.

She's been standing on her tip toes to see out of the window, so she's carefully getting down from the high bench seat, coming down backwards, her tiny feet searching for the ground beneath her. I'm sure she won't fall, but I'm such a pussy where she's concerned I rush over and grab her up, twisting her round and planting tiny kisses along her forehead. She breaks out into that giggle of hers, a few heads turn to see where it's coming from, and every one of these tough ass bikers breaks out in a smile when they see it's her.

"You want to play outside, princess?" I've hardly finished the sentence before she squeals her reply, right in my goddamn ear - almost deafening me. I gently let her down and she grabs hold of my hand and Disney's, walking between us, trying desperately to get us to swing her between us. Ice and a couple of other brothers follow us out, they've all fallen for my princess and they want to watch over her. Or maybe they want the fresh air too.

I count to three and she squeals even louder as Disney and I pull her up in a swinging motion. By the time we've reached the back door of the clubhouse my arm feels like it's about to be pulled out of the socket. From the look of Disney he's feeling it too.

Elizabeth releases both of our hands as soon as we get outside. She rushes over to the play area, and then comes to a sudden halt. Her head turns one way, then the other. I'm confused until I realize she's just trying to decide which piece of play equipment to try out first.

She opts for the swing. Disney perches on one of the picnic tables, watching me push her higher and higher. He smiles as her squeals of joy get louder the higher she goes. She soon tires of the swings, then the slide and sandpit, before moving over to the roundabout and asking me to join her. That means Disney has to get up and push us. Elizabeth chooses not to sit on her own but crawls into my lap and snuggles close, shouting at

Disney to push us round faster each time we come back round to where he's standing.

Her little cheeks are red from all the excitement and running she's been doing/ I know she'll fight it but her eyes are starting to show she's tired. She's so little she still needs an afternoon nap. Eve will give me hell if I don't put her down soon. She's got a bit of Eve's temper in her and she can be a right little diva when she's overtired.

Disney stops pushing at my unspoken signal, slowing the roundabout down. Before it's totally finished turning, I grab Elizabeth tightly and launch us off it. Another squeal. I need to start wearing ear defenders around this kid!

As I cradle her close, heading back to our room she squeezes me tightly. "Angel my new Daddy?"

Shit. I'm not sure how to respond to that. It's a conversation Eve and I still need to have.

"Not yet, Princess." I try to be diplomatic for her little ears. "But I'd like to be one day, when you and your mummy are ready."

She thinks about it a little, and then smiles before reaching up and planting a wet kiss on my cheek. She snuggles closer; I can see her eyes closing before we've even reached the end of the hallway.

Chapter Eighteen

Diane

I'm getting a new tattoo today; I'm really looking forward to it, as with all my tattoos I've gone for something that means something to me. I'm having a design I put together myself, it's a phoenix rising from the ashes into the sun on my right arm and some script on the back of my shoulder.

Ink hasn't been himself the past few days and I'm going to find out why while we're in the tattoo room together. I like the girl he brought back from England with him. Elle seems like a good match for him, Eve loves her which is a good sign for me, but part of me worries that Elle is too good for this life. Ink has demons he never shares, and because of that he never stays with a girl long. If I didn't know better I'd say he feels like he doesn't deserve to be happy with a woman. He's a great guy, and it saddens me when I see him hang around with the club whores. He needs an old lady to settle him down, to silence any demons he thinks he has. I'm going to see what I can do to make that happen for him.

Ink shows me the template on my arm and I love it. This is going to be one cool looking tattoo. The color's I've chosen are vibrant and celebrate life.
"I love it, what do you think?" I ask him. He's been more withdrawn than usual today; I'm struggling to get anything out of him.

"It's a cool design, Dragon will love it." He replies.

"Fuck Dragon." I laugh. "I'm getting it done for me, not him. If he likes it then cool, if he doesn't then he'll just have to live with it." I may love my husband but I'm still my own person, old lady or not.

Ink finally cracks a smile at that. "Bet you don't say that to his face." He smirks. He knows me too well. I don't answer Dragon back, much. I save it for the times I know it will provoke a reaction, and that's in the bedroom. I'm momentarily distracted from talking to Ink with thoughts of cuffs, whips and spreader bars but I snap myself back to the present.

"Tell me about Elle? She seems pretty cool." As soon as I mention Elle's name his face shows guilt. What's the stupid fuck done now? He says nothing, pretending to concentrate on working the needle on my skin.

"Ink, what the fuck was that look about? What have you done now you crazy biker?"

He pauses, wiping away the excess ink with a cloth, refusing to look me in the eye whilst he does it.

"Ink." I'm much more forceful this time.

"Diane, I fucked up. I think I fucked up big time." His face falls.

"Oh Ink, what have you done? I'm sure we can fix it sweetie." I reach over with the arm he isn't tattooing and gently pat him on the back. "Come on; tell me all about it and I'll see what we can do."

The truth comes out slowly. He's hesitating to tell me, but I can sense it involves another woman.

"This chick came in for a tattoo the other day, real cool chick. Had a history behind her tattoo, and we got to talking about it. She was a looker, and easy to talk to. She came onto me, not like with the club whores, she was classy with it. She said no strings, she was just after sex. I'm a guy, Diane. What could I do?" He pauses, crestfallen. "It's not like me and Elle are going anywhere, we both know we're just enjoying the sex whilst it lasts, so it wasn't like I was cheating. We've never said we were going steady or anything." He pauses again. I think he's trying to convince himself of the truth of his words rather than me. Stupid man can't see what's happening right in front of his face. Elle really could be into him if he gave her the chance.

"Anyway, one thing led to another and we had some pretty hot sex." His eyes look down to the table I'm sat on and I cast a disgusted look. He blushes and I see a hint of a smile. "I cleaned it off properly Di!" He protests. Then his eyes flicker to the wall. He's obviously replaying another memory. This sounds like it was a little more serious than a quick fling.

"Anyway, as soon as we were done with her tattoo she got up and left."

"What about Elle?" I'm guessing that as he hasn't got a black eye she doesn't know about this. She doesn't strike me as the type to accept this kind of behavior, casual relationship or not.

"I haven't told her." He looks to me, sighing heavily. "I'm torn mate, part of me says I respect her enough to tell her, and the other part of me say's it's none of her business who I put my dick in." The first part of that comment is the Ink I know and love, the second half is the biker talking.

There's a huge bang as the door flies fully open, causing me to jump. Ink tenses, I turn to see a very pissed off Elle. She's obviously heard our conversation. Fuck, I'm so glad Ink had removed the tattoo gun from my arm before the crash.

"You fucking bastard!" Elle rushes across the room, fists clenched, her face hard and pissed off. She stands right in front of Ink. I sensibly move away a little to give them some space. "I thought I was a little more than a casual fuck, or am I just somewhere to stick your dick, like all the others!" She screams. Wow, this girl sure can shout.

Just as I suspected, she lets loose with her hands, giving him such a hard slap across the face that I can feel the sting. That's going to leave a mark.

"Elle. I was going to tell you, honest babe. It meant nothing." Ink holds Elle's hands down by her side to stop her flying fists.

"Well it meant something to me, you fucker! You've been balls deep in my pussy every day since we met, it's not like you needed to look elsewhere for it. I mean fucking hell, Ink! You fucked me so hard the other night because you were jealous of Ice flirting with me! How would you feel if I went off and fucked him?" Ink suddenly looks pissed, without needing to hear his words we all know that Ink wouldn't like that at all; but she's right. Why should he have all the fun and Elle not have any, if they're not serious?

"So why? What don't I have that she has?" Elle is losing a little of her fire now. Instead, she's starting to look defeated and broken.

"It's not like that Elle, the opportunity was there and I just couldn't resist. I'm sorry babe; I've tried to tell you. I wanted to tell you, but I didn't want to hurt you." Ink's eyes show the sadness he's feeling. This girl means more to him than he realizes.

"Too late Ink, I won't be anyone's sloppy seconds. The sex was good but I can't, and won't, put up with you whoring around. I'm out of here." Elle turns quickly, giving me a quick look of apology as she passes. She slams the door behind her as she leaves.

"Aren't you going after her?" I ask. Ink shakes his head.

"I'll give her time to calm down first, besides I've got your tattoo to finish." I think he's making a mistake, but I don't correct him. I just hope for his sake she's still here when he's ready to go fix things.

Ink picks up the tattoo gun and continues where he left off, coloring the rising sun on my arm.

Elle

I'm such a stupid cow!

Ink never made me any promises. I know that. He never said he'd be faithful, hell he's a biker. Does he even know what faithful means?

I thought with the occasional jealous fits he's shown, that something was happening between us. I guess I was wrong.

Tears are streaming down my face as I enter the room we've been sharing since we got back.

Quickly I grab my bag, stuffing everything into it haphazardly. Walking into the bathroom I sweep my toiletries from the shelf straight into the bag, uncaring whether I ruin my clothes or not. I contemplate taking the sexy lingerie I bought to wear for him, but decide against it. I don't want that memory anymore. The best thing for me is to forget all about Ink.

I take one last look at the bed where we made love this morning, his betrayal catching in my throat.

I can't forgive him. I'm out of here.

Chapter Nineteen

Eve

Ink has been so down since Elle left. Neither of them has told me what happened. I think Diane knows but she's keeping tight lipped. It's not like her to gossip, well not unless it's about the club whores anyway.

Its lunchtime and Ink's just come in from working in the shop in town; he looks drained. I call him over to the bar where I'm sitting. Angel's gone off on some errand and I'm too nosey not to take this opportunity to find out what's been happening. Besides, I care for them both. They've become really good friends of mine.

"You want to tell me what's going on?" I ask him directly. He gives me a pained look, before pulling up a stool and sitting next to me. The prospect on duty quickly appears, passing him a beer and topping up my cola. It's too early for me to be drinking.

"Basically, I fucked up," he sighs loudly, looking over at me. "I fucked up big time, Eve. I didn't realize what I could have had. There was this great woman right in front of my eyes and I threw it away in a moment. I was thinking with my dick instead of my head, and now Elle's gone. She won't talk to me; I've fucked it all up before it even began." Ink's never given me the impression he's a man whore, but from the odd comment the guys make, I do know he's not into repeat performances. It's why I was so surprised to see Elle return from England with him.

We spend some time talking about how he feels about Elle. I can see he's scared that he has any feelings for her at all. He'd thought it was just some hot sex for the both of them and was making the most of it while it lasted. From what Elle had told me in our earlier chats I'd thought she was on the same wavelength as him as well.

Ink took advantage of Emma's offering herself up with no strings. It was something he'd not have thought twice about before Elle, but he thinks there's more between him and Elle than just sex. There's a connection there he's not had before. He's quick to protest that he doesn't love her. He's pretty vague when he says he's not even sure he knows what love is. That's a conversation I want to dig into deeper, but he's too resistant. He tries to change the topic but I won't let him. It's obvious this guy has some demons in his past, but he's not going to share them with me today.

He tells me about Elle's reaction to his possessiveness the night they arrived. That sounds like Elle. I think she'd have reacted like that even if they were together properly. She's quite strong and independent bless her. I can see how he'd misunderstand that. I try and explain that even though I'm Angel's old lady I'd be pissed if he spoke about me like that. Just because these guys are alpha bikers, they shouldn't talk about women like that. I try to help him understand that Elle and I weren't raised around the biker lifestyle. While his behavior may have been considered a compliment by someone like Diane, personally I can see why Elle was pissed off. To me it's like a dog pissing on a tree to mark his territory. There's nothing romantic about that. It's just macho bullshit.

Ink was the one person who stood by me when Elvis died, he was there for me. If I can help him resolve this situation with Elle, I will.

"You're off back to work this afternoon aren't you?" He nods. "Let me call Elle and see if I can get her to come over and have a chat. I'm not sure I'll be able to persuade her to come back here, but I'll play the boredom card. Guilt her into it if I have to." A smile starts to light up his face.

"You'd do that for me?" What happened to this guy that he seems so pleased by my small gesture?

"I'll do it for both of you. Elle is my friend as well, and right now, she's the only friend I have outside of this fucked up lifestyle I seem to have landed myself in."

I'm not just doing it for him. I need to speak to someone outside of the club, and as I'm forbidden to leave the compound my options are limited. I can't believe Angel used the word forbidden with me. It was like a red rag to a bull. He blustered his way through an apology, trying to convince me it was for my safety. I finally forgave him, but that was days later after he finally gave in and made love to me. I'd forgive that man anything after a hot session in bed.

I blush, drawing my attention back to Ink and away from the hot scenes I'm re-enacting in my head. He gives me a knowing smirk.

"You're thinking about Angel aren't you?" He laughs. Damn, was I that obvious?

"So..." I try to get our conversation back on track. "Do you want me to call her or not?"

"If you can get her to give me another chance I'll be your friend forever." He smiles.

"Ink, you were gonna be my friend forever anyway." I laugh. "I'll see what I can do."

Ink gets up from his chair, pausing to give me a kiss on the cheek. I'm glad Angel isn't around to see it, innocent as it was. He still has a bee in his bonnet over me getting close to Ink on my last trip out here.

"I'm glad you're back, babe." Ink hugs me. "You're good for this club." He grabs his keys from the bar, and heads back to work.

I pull out my phone, wondering what's the best way to start this conversation with Elle. I decide to chicken out and text her instead.

EVE: Hey babe, I'm dying of boredom here. Any chance you could come over this afternoon?

ELLE: Will Ink be there? I don't want to bump into him.

EVE: Nope, he's at the shop in town, won't be back till late.

ELLE: In that case, yes, see you in an hour xx

I'm looking forward to seeing my friend again. I hope she and Ink can work out whatever this is between them. I can see it from both sides, and feel a little like I'm stuck in the middle here. I don't want to lose Elle though; over here she seems to be my only connection with the real world.

I look at the clock and notice it's time to go rescue Teresa. She's been looking after Elizabeth this morning, and if I know my daughter they'll both be worn out.

Chapter Twenty

Eve

Elle takes just over an hour to get to the Severed MC clubhouse. Heads turn as she walks in. Her long blonde hair looks perfect as always. She's wearing black shorts that show off those fabulous legs of hers, and a plain white shirt. I can tell she's a little nervous and unsure as she looks around the room. As soon as she spots me sitting at the bar her face breaks out in a huge smile. I rush over to give her a hug.

"God I missed you." She says into my ear, hugging me back.

"How are you?" We both sit on bar stools, facing each other.

"Better now I've seen you. I've been bored shitless."

I laugh, but see she's deadly serious. "You can come see me anytime."

She gives me a look. I know what she's going to say. "Yeah right, when I can bump into him whilst I'm here. Sounds fabulous."

The prospect approaches us to take our order, but we don't want anything to drink. I suggest going somewhere quiet, and with more privacy than here. Angel is out on club business, and Elizabeth is down for a nap in

Teresa's room after watching one of Teresa's many Disney films on DVD. I decide the best place is mine and Angel's room.

"Where are we going?" Elle asks when I tell her to follow me.

"My room, we need to talk."

"We are talking."

I turn to look at her. She knows what I'm going to say. "We need to really talk Elle, alone."

She sighs, nodding her head, then following me to my room. When I shut the door we sit on my bed, facing each other, our legs crossed.

"Ok, honey. I think it's time we had a heart to heart."

Elle bites on her bottom lip. I hate the shine that appears in her eyes, but she nods her head.

"He hurt me, Eve." She sniffles a little. "I went to surprise him while he was at the shop. When I got there I overheard him telling Diane how he fucked some random woman. He fit her in for a quickie before doing her tattoo! I mean, for fucks sake! Who does that shit?"

I place my hand on her knee as she swipes away the tears that are threatening to fall.

"I thought we were going somewhere. I know he's not the settling down type, but I had this feeling that we'd connected. Obviously I was wrong."

"He does care about you." I protest.

"Not enough to keep his dick out of another woman." She looks up to the ceiling, raking her fingers through her blonde locks. "I just want to belong somewhere, Eve. I know it sounds really pathetic, but I've never been wanted by anyone. Nobody ever wanted me, not even my parents."

I stay silent, Elle hasn't told me her life story yet. I gathered she was a private person and was happy to wait until she was ready.

"An hour after I was born, I was placed in care. My mother didn't even want me for a day, she just gave me away." She pauses, and I pass her a box of tissues. She takes one, blowing her nose loudly before continuing. "I grew up in a shitty children's home, eventually moving from foster home to foster home. Even the foster families didn't want to keep me. They just wanted the paychecks. I was an unwanted burden for everyone. I was beaten nearly every day in my teen years." She sees the question in my eyes before I can ask it. "No, I was never sexually abused; it was just beatings and psychological abuse. Forever being told I was useless and ugly. Told I wasn't wanted. I was dressed in unfashionable and threadbare hand me downs, so I was pretty much a loner all through school." Tears stream down her face now. I try and hold my own back. "To this day I'm still a loner. I struggle to bond with people, but as soon as I met you, Eve, I just knew, I felt a connection with you I've never felt before. You're my first real friend."

She smiles but it's full of tears and mine fall freely. I can't hold back anymore after she said that. I really feel for her. I know our friendship was very sudden, but I think it's because we somehow recognized the broken part of each other. It helped us bond. I can't imagine how bad my childhood would have been if I hadn't had Teresa and her family. Whilst my mother wouldn't win any mother of the year awards, at least she'd kept me. Elle had nobody. I scoot over, holding her as she cries. When she's calmed down she looks at me.

"I want a family Eve. I want to have children, give them what I never had. I didn't think that I wanted that until I met you, and saw what you had. I'm so jealous of your life right now." She scoffs a little. "Well apart from the evil twin part."

We both laugh a little at that.

"Honey, you will always have me in your life."

"Yeah, I know." She lets out a deep, heavy breath. "For a moment there, I actually thought Ink might be the man to give me that. Obviously not."

"Elle, I think you need to have a chat with Ink." She shoots me a hard glare. "Hear me out. I spoke to Ink this morning. He's been miserable since you left. He knows he fucked up." She's about to protest but I continue. "I'm not agreeing with what he did. I'm furious at him for what he did, but I think deep down he's got some demons of his own. You two need to sit down and talk it through."

She shakes her head at me. "Ink isn't the settling down type, Eve. The sex was amazing," she blushes a little at the memory. "But seeing what you have, and realizing it's what I want, means I need to find someone who can give me that. That's not Ink, I thought for a second it could be, but when I heard what he'd done I knew he's the wrong man for me."

We pull apart. I smooth down her hair the same way I do with Elizabeth when she's upset. "You need to say all this to him babe, he needs to hear it. He needs to talk to you too, tell you what is haunting him, and what he wants from the future."

She stands up from the bed, straightening herself out. "I need time to think about it. I promise I'll ring him tomorrow though."

I stand and smile. "Good."

We walk out arm in arm, stopping in the bar for a quick drink before she goes. We're still gossiping about Ink when Ellen, one of the old ladies overhears us and wanders over.

"God that man is delicious, don't you girls tell my old man, but just looking at Ink makes my foo foo clench real hard."

Elle and I almost choke on our drinks, we're laughing so hard at her comment. I tell Ellen to bugger off so we can gossip. Ellen grins as she walks off to join her old man.

***

I'm sitting on a bench out back of the clubhouse with Teresa when I spot Preacher stomping across the yard, a furious look on his face.

Oh no, this can't be good. When there's drink around, Preacher can get in a really touchy mood.

I look at who he has his eyes set on; almost laughing out loud when I see he's headed for our newest member, Justice.

Justice is minding his own business, flirting with a few of the club women. Most of them are single, daughters of members or their friends, but there's one who's very much taken. The pretty red head who's laughing along with the rest of them is non-other than Rose, Preachers old lady.
Oh, shit.

Justice has his back to Preacher, but as he makes his way over everyone stops to see the reason behind Preacher's sudden change of mood. They snicker and smile, following behind him.

"Shit's about to go down." Teresa whistles.

"Maybe we should get Angel or Prez."

Teresa shakes her head and stands. "No way, let's go watch. I've been dying to see how Justice handles himself." She wiggles her eyebrows suggestively.

"I dunno."

She reaches for my hand, dragging me up from the bench. "Come on, if it gets out of hand I promise to get Prez."

She puts on her most innocent face, she's not fooling me. She won't fetch Prez I know that for certain, but I am a little curious, so I let Teresa lead me over to the growing crowd.

By now Justice has turned to face Preacher and the girls have disappeared into the growing crowd. Rose is standing behind her old man, where she should have been a moment ago. If there's one thing I've learned around here, it's that the men are very protective of their women. So if a sexy new member like Justice arrives and is holding your old ladies attention, you're going to remind everyone of your claim on her.

Justice stands with his arms crossed, frowning at Preacher who's standing right in front of him. He's shouting and pointing his finger in Justice's face.

"You leave my woman alone boy! Just 'cause you're Prez's nephew don't mean you're anything special."

"I didn't say I was Preacher." Justice says, already sounding bored of the whole situation.

Preacher lowers his finger, not knowing what else to say. Preacher is a big man; he's not as tall and stacked as Justice though. Preacher's a little softer in places, but he's still an attractive man and rocks the whole biker image. I wouldn't want to get on the wrong side of either of these men.

"Just stay the fuck away or I'll have to do something."

"Like what?" Justice asks, taunting Preacher. He turns his gaze to Rose and winks at her. "We're good friends ain't we Rosey?"

Rosey?

I hear Teresa giggling quietly, I want to join her. Rose bites on her lip and blushes. I'm not the only one to notice, Preacher shrugs off his leather cut. Wrong move Rose.

Justice smiles widely as he slowly removes his black shirt, revealing a marvelous ripped upper body. Every woman's gaze zeros in on Justice, including Rose and that finally does it for Preacher.

He charges towards Justice, raising his fist in the air and landing it straight on Justice's jaw. I wince as Justice rubs his jaw. That had to hurt.

Surprisingly Justice just smiles at Preacher. "I'll let you have that one out of respect for your old lady, but you don't get any more, that's my final warning."

He looks at Preacher seriously, but Preacher ignores him. He goes in for another hit, but Justice blocks it landing one of his own on Preacher's eye. Fists fly as they pound away at each other.

"And the game begins." Teresa sing songs.

I look at her in confusion so she points over to two members who are exchanging money. There are others in the crowd doing the same. Are they betting?

"How 'bout you Tess?" A voice comes behind us. I turn to see Ice standing there, his hand full of money.

Teresa reaches into her pocket. "Gotta go with Justice." She says, handing him some money.

Ice raises his eyebrows, and shrugs. "I dunno, I'm going with my man Preach, he's got a good arm."

Ice indicates over our shoulders. I turn back to see Preacher land a hard punch in Justice's stomach. I grimace as Justice bends over from the force of the hit, but he's back up quickly. He pushes Preacher to the floor, landing a hit right on Preachers nose.

"How about you, Eve?" Ice asks. I shake my head.
"Go on Justice!" Teresa shouts from beside me. I look at her in shock.

This is fucking madness.

Justice gets up; it gives Preacher a chance to get up as well. Every woman's eyes go straight to Justice's sexy chest. He's all sweaty now, so the light glistens off him, making his abs and tattoos look shiny and emphasizing them even more.

Preacher charges at Justice and they're at it again, everyone chanting for their favorite fighter. Just then there's a loud shout.

"What the fuck!"

Prez charges down the yard and lands straight in the middle of the fight. He pulls Justice off Preacher. I'm surprised Prez can lift a man that size. Preacher goes for Justice again but Gabe is there, holding him back.

"Now you two stop acting like kids and sort your shit!" Prez shoves Justice towards the bar while Gabe does the same with Preacher.

Is it really a good idea to point two men who were just fighting towards the bar for drinks? I don't think so, but I'm not going to intervene.

Prez walks in our direction. Ice discreetly gives Teresa her money back before walking away.

"Have fun?" Prez asks her, a smirk on his face.

"Thank god you broke that up Bill, I didn't think they would stop." She fakes. I don't buy that and I know Prez doesn't. He quirks an eyebrow at her then lifts her over his shoulders.
"Woman, do I need to remind you not to lie to me."

He walks off with an amused looking Teresa who gives me a thumbs up as she's dragged away, upside down.

"Like what you saw, princess?" I hear Gabe's voice.

I turn to see him frowning at me, arms folded. "What?"

"Enjoy watching the fight?"

I shake my head.

"Justice has a good body huh?"

Wait? Is Gabe jealous? Oh this is precious!

I try to hold in my smile, but it creeps through a little and I swear I hear Gabe growl.

The sound arouses me. I close the distance between us, placing my hand on his hard chest. "No baby, it's not a patch on yours."

His chest puffs out in pride. He kisses me long and hard for all to see. He presses his hard, jean covered cock into me and I moan. Suddenly I'm lifted over Gabe's shoulder and carried across the yard just like Prez did with Teresa.

"I'll show you just how good I am, princess." Gabe growls.

***

After three orgasms I am worn out. Gabe took me to the games room where he showed me just how much he loves me. Over, and over again. If this is how he treats me when he gets jealous, I might have to get him jealous more often!

He demanded I tell him I was his as he fucked me against the wall before taking me over the pool table. I was so scared someone would walk in, but in a way that excited me even more.

Gabe holds my hand and as we leave the games room I see Justice and Preacher sitting together on a bench. They both have beers in their hand, and are laughing together loudly.

"Wait! You're not shitting me?" I hear Preacher ask.

"Nope!" Justice answers. "After the girls stopped fighting, I suggested they share me and they did." He laughs.

Preacher shakes his head. "Five women, you lucky bastard!"

My eyes bug out of my head. Gabe leads me over to a table, pulling me down to sit down on his lap. Five women? Whoa!

Gabe starts to kiss along my neck and my mind shuts off. My hand travels up under his shirt. I feel the deep lines of his muscles hidden there. As much as I love it here and my new family, I can't wait for all this shit with Satan to be behind us so we can have our own place.

Chapter Twenty One

Elle

The morning after having my heart to heart with Eve, I feel refreshed and surprisingly good about everything.

I woke this morning knowing that Eve was right; Ink and I do need to talk. He needs to know what's going on in my head, and I need to know what the fuck's going on in his.

Drinking my second coffee I finally get the courage to send him a text.

Hey, we need to talk.

I don't have to wait long for my reply.

Sure, I'm at the clubhouse

I try to decide whether his text sounds good or bad, realizing I need to stop wasting time and get on with it. Strapping on my big girl pants, not literally because I don't need Ink to know I wear those, pissed off or not, I imagine pulling them up and march out to my car.

As I drive closer to where Ink waits for me, a nervous bug settles in my stomach. It only gets worse when I reach the gates, waving to Ice and

Rabbit who are standing guard as I pass. When I pass them I see him. Ink's leaning back against the clubhouse wall, one leg arched on the wall behind him. His arms are crossed; he has his dark sunglasses on. He looks dangerous. My heart breaks a little more at the memory of his betrayal, but my greedy pussy clenches with need.

Damn, Ink has my mind and body torn in two different directions.

I knew I cared for him before all this shit went down, but after crying over him so much, I realized somewhere along the line, I fell for him. It's too early to be love, but this is more than just lust.

Taking a deep calming breath, I grab my purse and get out the car. Ink stands straight as I make my way over, removing his shades. I watch as he takes me in. I high five my inner self at my choice of outfit. My frayed short denim skirt is paired with a tight vest top and my flip flops. I feel cool in this hot weather, and from the look on Ink's face, I look sexy too. Well done me!

"So, you finally ready to talk?" He asks.

"Eve persuaded me to hear you out." I quickly respond.

We stand awkwardly, just watching each other for a couple of minutes before Ink breaks the silence. "Let's go talk in my room."

He leaves quickly, I follow right behind. As soon as Ink closes the door behind me, he's on me in a flash. Lips tongue and hands are everywhere! My skirt has somehow managed to come up and reveals my lace thong. Yay for not actually wearing the big girl pants! Ink's hand wanders under my top, pinching my nipple.
"Ink." I manage to say in between kisses.

"Ink!" I shout, finally breaking through to him.

He lifts his mouth from mine but doesn't step away, or remove his hands from my breast and ass.

"What baby?"

"I'm here to talk."

"Yeah, we can." He kisses me. "After."

I push at his chest and try my firm voice. "Ink, for fucks sake, we need to talk!"

He finally steps away, huffing. He sits down on the bed, shaking his head. "Fucking women and talking."

I straighten myself out before joining him on the bed. He looks up at me through his dark lashes. "Sorry babe, but you look fucking hot and I've missed you." His hand slowly trails up my thigh. "God, I've fucking missed you."

I stop his hand from going any higher, and he smiles like a naughty school boy. He sits up and spreads out his arms. "I'm all ears."

"Why?"

His smile automatically falls, and he rubs his face, hard. "Fuck, I knew you'd want to talk about that."

"Damn right, Ink! You slept with someone else!"
He closes his eyes as though he's in pain. "I know, I fucked up, Elle. I know I did and trust me, I fucking hate myself for it."

"But why?"

"I don't know."

I stare into his eyes and I realize I made a huge mistake coming here. I get up to leave, but Ink stops me. Grabbing my wrist and moving closer.

"Where are you going?"

"Home. I'm done."

I see his eyes widen. He pulls me back down as I try and make another escape.

"Stay, please." He pleads." Don't go, Elle. I miss you."

"No, I think it's just the sex you've missed. So I'm just going to go."

I manage to stand this time. I only manage two steps before Ink pushes me back down on the bed and hovers over me. Searching my face.

"No, you're not just sex to me. Somehow, without even knowing it, you broke me."

My breath catches at his words. He sounds tormented.

"I never thought I wanted to settle down with one woman. Until I got to know you. If I'm honest Elle, you scare the shit out of me." He laughs a little, wiping away the few tears that have fallen from my eyes.

He leans in close, lightly brushing his lips over mine. "I could love you."

My eyes open wide. "I fell for you a long time ago, I should have said something but I couldn't. I've never experienced loving someone Elle. Friends, yes but not like this. Like I am with you. You own me."

He leans back down and without another thought, I let him kiss me and take me away. He rips away our clothes and gives me the pleasure only he can give me, because sex with Ink is deeper than with anyone else. We connect. As he thrusts harder, he looks right into my eyes and tells me again that he could love me.

"I could love you too." I whimper back. It might be too early for love, but I'm pretty certain that's where this is heading for both of us.

Ink pauses for just a second, then before fucking me harder than he has ever done before.

***

When we're both fully sated and lying face to face on his bed we finally talk a little more. I tell him everything I told Eve yesterday, about my life growing up. I'm surprised when Ink tells me about his childhood. Apart from the foster care, he pretty much suffered the same. Only his was worse. Ink was homeless, having to fight for his survival on a daily basis. The only love he's ever received or given is with his club brothers, and now me. Right now I've forgiven Ink for sleeping with another woman. It was really wrong of him to do it, but in a weird way I understand what was going through his head. He was scared of what we are becoming. Without thinking he tried to subconsciously ruin us. Only, it's made us stronger.

"So what are we?" I ask him, lazily trailing my fingers over his sculptured chest.

"You're mine babe." He responds.

"As in your girlfriend?" I laugh, but I'm deadly serious.

He leans down, kissing my forehead. "As in, being my one and only woman."

He pushes me down into the bed and shows me just how Ink treats his one and only woman.

***

After a long night of very hot make up sex I wake up, wrapped in the comfort of Ink's arms. We decided last night that we'll give it a go as a couple. Ink's asked me to move in to the clubhouse with him, both of us want to see if this is leading where we think it is. We're both scared; neither of us has experienced anything like this before. After just a few days apart though, we think it's worth the risk.

Ink's place is here, with the club. Because I'm always travelling, my house feels more like a hotel than a home. There are no special memories there, no reason for me to stay away from Ink any longer. Ink's got a full day of work today at his shop in town, and it will take me all day to pack my things and put the house in order. I'll keep renting it, just in case, but I'll be moving my things to the clubhouse tomorrow. Ink's going to send one of the prospects over in the morning with a truck, and I'll drive my car back here so I've got it when I need it.

I'll miss being in Ink's bed tonight, but I console myself with the knowledge that every night after this that's where I'll be. I get a lovely warm feeling, and reach over to shake Ink awake. I need him to remind me what I'll be missing tonight.

Chapter Twenty Two

???

Shit!

I look down at my phone when I hear the incoming text alert and see that it's from him. I don't want to open the message in here, but it will look suspicious if I go outside to read it. I glance around the room; no one seems to be taking any notice of me. A couple of the guys are playing poker over in the corner, some more are playing on the Xbox, and Prez is safely in his office - I hope.

The icon tells me it's a picture message. I pause for a moment before sliding across the screen to open it. If it's coming from him it's bound to be unpleasant. I take a deep breath to prepare myself for what I'm about to see.

Fuck!

It's another picture of my sister, and from the image in the background I know it's been taken today. That means he's there. I scroll down the image to see his message.

What's taking so long?
Be a shame to have to talk to your sister.

Call me...

I'm seething with rage, but trying to keep a handle on it. I wish I knew what to do. Part of me says to go tell Angel and Prez, to fess up and ask for their help. I'm sure they'd understand with it being Satan. But the other part of me tells me I'd be signing my death warrant. If the club doesn't kill me for betraying them, then Satan sure as fuck will, and he'll hurt my sister as well, just for the fun of it. I can't even think of any way of leading the club to Satan so they can get him. The sneaky bastard never tells me where he is, and all I have contact wise is the crappy pre-paid phone number he's using. I never know when he'll next be in touch or where he'll pop up.

I need to get out of here somehow and make this call. Find out what the fucker wants now. I also need to reign my temper in before I talk to him, I need to be damned careful I don't say something that I'll regret later, something he'll take out on my sister.

***

Angel

Each day that goes by knowing that Satan is still out there is eating away at my soul. I feel weak, I'm the man, I'm supposed to keep my family safe and right now I don't even know what direction the threat is going to come from.

Half the MC's in Australia are helping us try and locate him. He's pissed most of them off over the last few years so there's no shortage of willing volunteers. I'm pretty sure he's somewhere local. Knowing that sick fucker he'll be close by, watching, and just waiting for an opportunity to strike.

Prez has called me to his office to go over some club business we need to deal with. I pass through the common room as I go. It's fairly quiet in here today, a lot of the guys are out working or running club errands but I see a handful still here. Cowboy is in a corner, playing on his phone, a real pissed off expression on his face. I wish the dumb fuck would realize he sucks at Candy Crush and just find another game to play. Ice and Cherry are on the Xbox. I smirk as I realize the combination of their names sounds like something you'd ask for in a girly fucking cocktail.

Eve and Elizabeth are sleeping in our room. Eve seems to need a lot more rest since her accident and losing the baby. I know she's frustrated that I won't let her leave the compound; I just can't take the risk. At least whilst she's behind these gates I know she's safe.

I reach Prez's office door and knock at the same time as I push the door open. As I enter I see Prez leaning over a very flustered looking Teresa. Hearing my knock they stop what they're doing and laugh. Prez sucks his fingers as Teresa quickly adjusts her dress. I'm feeling very fucking awkward right now. When will he learn to lock his fucking door?

Prez smacks Teresa hard on the ass as she goes to leave, giving me a cheeky wink as she passes. She shuts the door behind her and I look up to see Prez wearing a shit eating grin. I shake my head. "You need to lock the fucking door Prez."

He just sits in his big chair and laughs. "Seriously Prez, you two are getting as bad as Di and Dragon."

That makes him laugh even harder. When he's stopped I sit down opposite him to get down to business. Time for the men to talk.

***

???

I thought Angel was going to catch me then as he walked through the common room, but he didn't acknowledge me. He either saw me and didn't think to say anything or didn't see me at all. I'm hoping that he didn't see me. I give myself a quick shake, trying to get my head in the right place. I'm going to have to call Satan and get this over with.

I head for the front door, shouting over my shoulder to ask the guys if anyone needs anything bringing back from the store. They're so engrossed in what they're doing that mostly I just get negative grunts in response.

I finger my keys in my pocket as I head to my bike. For the first time in as long as I can remember I'm not looking forward to this ride. I feel like the net is closing in.

***

I wipe my mouth with the back of my hand. What I heard on that call made me throw up like a fucking girl, all over the dusty ground. I'm not sure if that's bile I can taste in the back of my throat, or betrayal.

Satan has upped the ante. He's tired of waiting for Eve, so instead he's going to take Angel out. And he needs my help to do it. I've got to lure Angel to a meeting point, come up with some story about having a lead on Satan's location to get him there. Angel's so fired up right now if I can catch him alone I know he'll go out there solo. He won't wait for Prez and the guys to talk through a plan; he'll just jump right in and finish it.

If I do this, I'm signing Angel's death warrant. I don't even want to know what sick and twisted ending Satan has planned for him. I can't breathe. My chest feels like it's clamped in a vice. The more I think about betraying

Angel, the tighter it gets. I slide my phone open, looking at the picture message Satan sent me this morning. I have to do this. I have to save her. Angel is like a brother to me, but he's not blood. I have to save my baby sister if I can.

I get back on the bike, no longer relishing the speed. Every second takes me closer to the ultimate betrayal.

***

The common room is empty when I return. At this time of day I'm guessing most of the guys are at work or eating out back. I need to find Angel, ideally get him on his own. I can't risk anyone overhearing us. I'm just trying to work out how to do this when I slam into a body.

Fuck, it's Angel. I didn't see him walking down the corridor towards me. I pause for just a second. This is my last chance to pull out and come clean, but I can't. I open my mouth and start the conversation that is going to lead to the death of the man standing in front of me.

"Angel, glad I bumped into you." He laughs, as we literally did bump into each other. "I've had word from one of my snitches on a possible location for Satan. Do you want me to go check it out?" I know this man. There is no way he will let anyone else take on this task. I hope I know him anyway.

"Fuck, no. I'll check it out. How good is this information?" I swear I see the man increase in size. He hasn't of course, but the thought of a possible location for Satan has straightened his back. I don't think I'd noticed how slumped he's been since they came back from England. It's almost like the fight had been knocked out of him, but now it's back.

"You're not going alone, VP." A voice commands from behind me.

Fuck. This is just what I don't need. It's Prez and he's overheard our conversation. "Go with him, cover his back." He turns to Angel, a stern look on his face.

"I know how much you want to end this brother, but I'm telling you now. You do nothing more than check this out. If he's there, you call back here and we'll put a proper plan together. We'll go in prepared. Promise me you won't try and do this all on your own." He has his hand on Angel's shoulder during the exchange. Angel looks pissed, but he's too loyal to disobey his president and close friend.

"Fine. But if he is out there, we act tonight. I'm not waiting any longer than that; I'm not giving that fucker chance to escape."

Angel turns, and without any more words he strides to the front door and his bike, not even bothering to check if I'm following.

What have I done?

Not only have I betrayed my brother, now I'm pretty sure I'll be forced to watch him die.

Right now I wish I was dead.

Chapter Twenty Three

???

My instructions from Satan are to lead Angel to a secluded area a couple of hours away from the compound. It's down a sparsely wooded road in the middle of bloody nowhere. I'm a little unsure how he plans to get one over on Angel, the guy's hyper alert these days.

I managed to sneak a quick text letting him know we're on our way when Prez followed us out and distracted Angel for me, just before we left. Satan had seemed pretty certain I'd find a way of following through. I suspect his trap, whatever it is, would be in place even if I hadn't let him know.

I can't get my head around how two brothers can be such different characters. They're the spitting image of each other; although to me there's always been a sly, evil look about Satan. Angel's normally a pretty easy going and happy guy. Despite what happened in his past. Eve seemed to cure him of his nightmares when she came out here. He thinks no one knew about them, but several of us would hear him screaming himself awake most nights. We never let on; it wouldn't have been right. We couldn't take a guy's pride away from him like that.

I think about the number of years I've known Angel, the things we've been through together.

Shit. I can't do this.

I don't know how to stop it though. I contemplate signaling him to pull over and just letting it all spill out. My concentration is shot, it shows in the way I'm handling the bike. Angel looks over, giving me a concerned look. I give him the thumbs up to show its all okay. Who am I kidding? This situation is never going to be okay.

***

Satan

I can't get this insane grin off my face. The text has come through letting me know Angel is on his way. Everything's in place.

Finally, I'm going to be rid of him. I'm not sure when I first started to hate him. It's just been that way for so long I couldn't tell you when or why it happened.

My mother insisted she didn't have favorites when we were growing up, but she fucking did. When she looked at Angel her face would light up. More often than not when she looked at me she had to hide a look of revulsion. She got really good at hiding her emotions after a while; but by then it was too late. I knew how she really felt about me. The more outrageous my behavior, the more she pulled away from me. In the end I guess I just went all out, wondering just what it would take to get a reaction from her. If it wasn't for the way she treated Angel, I'd swear the woman couldn't love.

I've always derived pleasure from screwing over Angel. I'd break his toys, torture and kill his pets, steal his friends by telling lies about him, and later I'd steal his women. I still savor the memory of Beth. That was a sweet afternoon. I don't know why the fucker blames me for her death. She's the one who took the razor to her wrists, not me. I'd planned to keep playing with her for a lot longer. The memory is sweet. I'd pull up the video on my phone, but I can't afford to take my attention from the road, they could be here any time if they've put their foot down and it's a clear run. Knowing Angel, he'll break every speed limit between the clubhouse and here to have his chance at revenge.

Back in York I'd seen his face when he spotted me just after I pushed Eve into the path of the train. Pure hatred. That was such a great feeling. I'd wanted to torment him some more by killing Eve before him, but the stupid bitch never leaves that bloody compound. And as cunning as I am, there's no way I'm breaking in. Despite the satisfaction I'd get from stealing her from under their noses, there's too much risk. I'm a better poker player than that. But with Angel gone, I have a better chance of getting my hands on her. Even with Angel dead, I can still hurt him by getting his girl.

I thought long and hard about how to kill Angel. I've pictured his death so many times through the years, every death imaginable, each more painful and slow than the last. Whilst I hate that today is going to be quick, and sadly painless, it's going to be so shocking for those left behind. Let's just say they won't be having an open casket viewing. I snicker to myself at that thought. The more I think about the plan, the more I like it. It will certainly send a message to all the pussy assed MC's around here not to mess with me.

***

???

Angel is riding ahead of me as instructed by Satan. It's his natural place anyway as VP. I don't know what Satan's got planned, but I'm to ensure that if there's more than one of us accompanying Angel, he has to be in the lead. All I can think of is some sort of ambush.

We pull off the main highway, onto a rutted dirt road. I can feel every rut and pothole through the bike. At the end of this road Satan will be waiting.

Trees either side of the road provide occasional shade. I'm guessing whoever lived here originally planted an avenue of greenery to welcome visitors. The trees are standing opposite each other in an artificial planting arrangement.

There's a funny noise ahead and I look over to Angel's bike. I'm sure that was a misfire? I hear it again, and before I can comprehend Angel has slowed down, falling behind me. Shit. I've got to get him ahead of me again.

I'm a few trees ahead of Angel now, and just as I'm thinking of slowing down I see something reflect ahead of me. It's at head height in the road; it must be the sun reflecting off something shiny on the roadside. I wonder if it's Satan's hiding place being revealed by a reflection from the blazing overhead sun.

Too late I understand why Angel had to be ahead of me. What hangs ahead in the road was meant for him. My last thought - "I'm sorry."

***

Angel

There's something not quite right with my bike. I can hear a misfire. I slow down to try and figure out the problem from the sound. My brother obviously hasn't noticed anything's wrong as he's just pulled ahead of me. I'm sure he'll stop in a moment and come back to see what's wrong.

I'm about to increase the throttle to see if that will clear whatever's blocking the fuel when I look up. There's a flash of light in front of me, I'm not sure what it is but suddenly I'm on high alert. I reach for my gun and am about to shout for my brother to stop when it happens. What 'it' is I have no fucking idea. I can't comprehend what my eyes are telling me. It's both gruesome and unimaginable!

One minute he's riding along on his bike as normal. The next, his bike starts weaving as though he's lost control. I see his body slumping forward over the handlebars, but what really freaks me out is the sight of his head. It drops to the ground, rolling back along the road towards me like a fucking football!

I pull up the bike, vomit rising in my throat. I've seen some shit in my time with the club, but nothing like this.

Fuck me!

What the fuck just happened?

When I've finished throwing up on the side of the road I open my phone, dialing Prez's number.

"Prez, get the guys out here now. It was a trap."
"Are you okay, Angel?" He asks; concern heavy in his voice.

"Yeah, I'm okay. My fucking bike started misfiring, saved my fucking life." I sigh heavily. "Best send the truck and a body bag though... Disney's dead." I hang up the phone and throw up what's left of the acid in my gut.

Chapter Twenty Four

Gabe

I step inside the clubhouse needing a fucking drink. I walk up to the bar where the prospect already has my drink waiting. I order a vodka shot as well, throwing it back, it hits the spot.

Fuck! I can't believe what happened back there!

I look around; the clubhouse is practically empty of brothers right now. Some of them are busy cleaning up the mess I've just narrowly escaped from, and the rest are trying to hunt Satan down. He must have been close by; he'd have wanted to watch me ride to my death.

I look around at the brothers who stayed behind to protect our families and our club. I rub the back of my neck as the image of Disney riding into the wire that killed him quickly flashes through my mind. Shit, if my bike hadn't misfired, that would have been me. I wouldn't be standing here. I wouldn't see Eve or hold Elizabeth in my arms again.

After downing another shot of Vodka I try to get a hold on my emotions. They're pretty fucking twisted right now. Disney is dead. I don't know if I should be pissed at his betrayal, or upset that my friend has died.

Disney has been here for a long fucking time. He didn't grow up around the club like Prez and I did, but he joined as a prospect only a few years after I made Vice President. He was a good fucking brother to me. Why the fuck would he betray us like that?

There has to be a good reason and I intend to find out what. With Satan behind it, my guess is some sort of blackmail. Nobody would help Satan willingly.

I've lost a friend, a fucking brother, but he turned out to be a filthy rat. He fucking sold us out! He was sending me to my death. Fuck!

I don't know what to think, but nobody deserves to die like that. Well, I can think of one person, but then he deserves something much worse than that.

I take a deep and heavy breath before making my way into the main area. It's where the TV is with sofas lining the walls. It's where the women spend most of their time when they're here.

I spot Eve straight away. She's on one of the sofas, curled up with her Kindle in her hands. Cowboy is on the leather chair nearest to her, Elizabeth on his knee. I smile at the sight of my family, a calm settling over me.

I see there's a cartoon film on the TV for Elizabeth's benefit, some of the guys watching it with a scowl. It's hilarious to see, a bunch of bikers watching a Disney film because this little girl wants to watch it. I knew she'd have them all eating out of her hands.

I look at my woman, my sexy and brave old lady. She's absorbed in her reading and has no idea I'm standing here watching her. She's wearing short, skimpy shorts so I can see her long, tanned legs. I know if I glide my hand from her ankle to her thigh, her skin will be silky smooth. My hand twitches in anticipation as I become eager to get closer. I let my eyes lazily drag up her beautiful body. Her plump breasts rising and falling as she breathes. My hands clench as I hold back from charging over there. When my eyes travel up to her face I see she's now looking at me, biting on her bottom lip as she holds my gaze.

My woman is looking very fuckable right now. After the shit day I've had I need her. Preferably naked and wet.

Without another thought or word, I walk right up to her, as I do she puts away her Kindle. I grab her hand pulling her up to me, claiming her lips with mine; savoring her sweet taste. She moans against me and I hear Cowboy laugh.

I break away from Eve to glare over at Cowboy, but then quickly smile. He's got a hand over Elizabeth's eyes.

As much as I want my woman right now, I can't. I've got to take care of business. I look to Cowboy; his back straightens when he sees the look in my eyes. "We need to talk. Best go to Prez's office, now". He puts Elizabeth down gently and stands. Eve looks at me; she can tell from my tone this is serious. I can't tell her yet; I need time to understand it myself.

I give her a gentle kiss. "I'll explain later baby." She nods, drawing Elizabeth to her side, needing her close. I guess it must be some sort of maternal instinct. "Take care of mummy for me, princess," I plant a soft kiss on Elizabeth's forehead, her little chest filling out with pride at the important task she's been given.

I take a long, hungry look at my girls before leading Cowboy away. How the fuck do I tell him his best friend is dead, never mind that he betrayed the club. Fuck! Let's just get this over with.

***

Cowboy is sitting on the sofa in Prez's office, tears streaming down his face. What I've just told him has reduced this hardened biker to a crying wreck. It's taken three attempts to get him to understand I'm telling him the truth, he just can't and won't believe his best friend would betray any of us.

Prez clears his throat, embarrassed at seeing Cowboy like this. He's one of the strongest of us. Saying that, Prez and I are hurting as well, although we were close to him, we weren't as close as him and Cowboy.

"I just don't understand why?" He draws in a deep breath, trying to compose himself, slowly returning to the man I know. "What the fuck could have caused him to turn on us like this. I'd rather die than betray you guys and I thought he felt the same." He looks down at his hands, as though in search of the answer.

"It has to be some form of blackmail, that's all that makes sense to me right now. But I can't think what it could be?" I look to Cowboy for the answer. He shakes his head, the suddenly something occurs to him and he sits up straight.

"Fuck! Cassie!" He shouts, starting to rise to his feet. Prez and I turn to look at each other, neither of understanding what he's talking about. Cowboy's about to rush from the room when I pull him back.

"Slow down brother and explain what's got you so worked up."
"It has to be his sister, Cassie." Prez and I shake our heads. I don't think either of us even knew Disney had a sister.

"Sister?" Prez asks.

"Yea, she's younger than him, she's away at college. He was so fucking proud of her for making something of her life, but he was always worried she wasn't safe. He hated she was so far away from his protection. Her college is hours away from here." He pauses. She's the only thing I can think of that could explain this. Have you got his phone?"

I shake my head. "Sorry! I was so fucked up I got out of there as soon as the crew arrived! never thought about it. I was too busy getting back here to check on my girls." Before I've finished speaking Prez is on the phone to Ice, directing him to look for the phone. I can hear the murmur of Ice's voice on the other end of the phone but not the words themselves. He's obviously asked a question as he goes quiet waiting for Prez's reply.

"No, clean up the scene and bury him out at the usual spot." Prez's voice isn't quite as strong as it normally is I understand why. He's just refused Disney a proper burial. There'll be no club funeral for him, no wake, his picture will be taken down from the members wall and burned. It will be as though he was never a part of us. Fuck, this hurts. No matter why though, he betrayed us. This is what happens to traitors.

Cowboy moves to protest but I put a restraining hand against his chest. Prez hangs up the phone, turning back to us.

"I'm sorry Cowboy, you know the rules."

"At least let me go tell his sister, make sure she's okay?" He's asking permission, but I'm pretty certain nothing either of us could say to him would stop him going right now. I feel his pain.

Prez nods his head. "Take one of the prospects with you, make sure you're well armed. Check in when you get there and let me know what's happening, if she needs help." Cowboy thanks him, rushing from the room. Prez turns to me.

"The cleanup crew will be back in an hour or so, I'm calling Church as soon as they get back, this shit is out of control, we need to stop it now." He slams his fist into the wall before storming from the room. I sink to the sofa, my head in my hands, wondering how the fuck we get out of this mess.

Chapter Twenty Five

Satan

I don't fucking believe it! That lucky fucker isn't dead. The wire strung between the trees worked perfectly, but it's taken out the wrong fucking biker. I raise my gun through the gap in the bushes, but I'm too far away to get a clear shot and end this once and for all.

Fuck!

From my vantage point I watched in horror as that rat Disney overtook Angel and ruined my fucking plans.

It saves me from having to get rid of him later I suppose, but it means now I'm working blind!

I'm so fucking frustrated and annoyed right now! I need to vent this anger on someone, luckily I know a pretty little blonde that needs taking care of. She's about an hour's ride away from here. I get on my bike and fire it up. My hands are shaking as I gun the throttle, shaking from sheer fucking frustrated anger. I spend the ride imagining what I'm about to do to her, my cock's hard within minutes and straining painfully against my tight denim jeans. There's nothing that turns me on more than hearing a woman scream, and inflicting pain, although I'm pretty sure I'll come in my pants when I finally get to watch Angel die.

During the ride I come up with another plan. This one even sweeter than the one I'm currently riding towards. I've been watching those bitches at Severed, and I know their weakness. I grin, I'm going to unleash hell on those stupid fuckers, and before tonight is out I'll have my revenge. Angel will be dead, and I'll have fucked his whore Eve senseless in front of him.

***

The open road turns into suburbs, I know where I'm going; I've spent a lot of time here lately. I follow the road around the estate, locating the building I want. At this time of day I'll find her here. I know her schedule inside out. I idle the bike at the kerb; looking through the large glass window. She's there, laughing with her friends, drinking some fancy assed coffee. Make the most of it love; it's the last time you'll get to do this.

I'm going to wait until she comes out. She always leaves earlier than her friends, and that's when I'll grab her. For now I ease off the bike, moving to the park bench over the road where I sit and watch her. I play with the blade of my knife; it's going to get very well acquainted with her pale skin soon.

***

She stands and starts to hug her friend's goodbye, picking up her bag and moving to the door. I move closer, deliberately bumping into her as she exits the coffee shop.

"I'm so sorry miss, I didn't see you there." I sound like a fucking pussy, but it's working.

She smiles at me. Fuck, she's beautiful. There's something about her. She's classier than the whores I usually fuck. I bet she's fucking tighter than them as well. I can't wait to stick my dick in that sweet ass of hers.

"It's okay, these things happen."

"I wonder if you could help me, I'm looking for Cassie. Her friend said she's normally down here at the coffee shop at this time of day. I'm afraid I've got some bad news for her about her brother."

I force my face to look crestfallen.

"What's happened to my brother?" She gasps, "I'm Cassie."

"Well miss, I'm sorry but your brothers been hurt in a motorbike accident. He's in a bad way. The club sent me to get you so I could take you to him."

She lets out a sob when I tell her about the accident, she looks around her as though seeking her friends, and I need to get her out of here before they see her through the window.

"We need to hurry miss, we've just about got time for you to grab a few things so you can stay a few days with him if you want."

I'm banking on her being a typical broad and wanting her stuff with her. I need to get her back to her apartment to carry out the rest of my plan.

"Okay, sure. Are we going on your bike? I guess I'll need to change as well."

She still in shock, looking down at the long floaty skirt she's wearing. I guide her over to the bike, helping her on, before turning and asking where she lives. She gives me some brief directions, it's only a few minutes away but I already knew that. I know nearly everything about her; I've been following her when I haven't been staking out the Severed clubhouse. I fire up the bike and set off in the right direction.

She holds on tight like I'm some fucking knight in shining armor; she doesn't see the evil grin that covers my face as we drive away.

*****

She fumbles with her key in the lock, so I take it from her. She was quiet on the bike, but knew what she was doing. I guess she spent a lot of time on the back of her brothers' bike growing up; she doesn't look like old lady material.

I let her move ahead of me into the apartment; she stumbles around for a moment or so then turns to face me.

"Sorry, I don't know what I'm doing. Make yourself comfy and I'll go grab a few things."

As soon as she's turned out of sight I lock the door behind us, putting on the safety chain. Shame it's not going to keep her safe this evening.

I move on silent feet down the hallway, through the open door I see her throwing clothes into a bag on her bed. She's crying quietly. She senses my presence and looks up at me.

"How bad is he?" I have to hold back my snicker, composing myself before I reply.

"He's pretty bad I'm afraid, but don't worry. I promise you'll be joining him before the evenings over."

She looks confused by my odd choice of words. I reach my hands into my leather jacket, curling my fingers around the familiar object. Her eyes grow wide. She stands straight as she watches me pull out my knife. I smile at her, advancing into the room and shutting the door behind me.

Chapter Twenty Six

Cowboy

My heart is thumping as I make my way to Cassie's. I can't believe what Angel and Prez have just told me. Disney was like a brother to me, we were damned close. Obviously we weren't as close as I thought or he'd have come to me. I hope I'm wrong, but the only thing I can think of that would persuade Disney to betray the club is Cassie.

I haven't seen her for years now; Disney liked to keep her away from the club. He wanted better for her than us old farts, can't say I blame him. She'll be late teens or early twenties now from memory. I remember him telling me when she'd been accepted to college. He was so damned proud. She's getting some sort of marketing degree I think. I know he fell out with his parents over her choice of college; he wanted her to stay closer to home so he could keep an eye on her, but they let her go where she wanted. He's a typical big brother.

I pause and take a deep breath.

He was a typical big brother. He'd tease the shit out of her, but woe betides anyone who even looked at her the wrong way.

I can't get my head around it, not only is he gone, but he's being buried in secret like a criminal. No service for us to say goodbye, or remember him.

I won't even be allowed to mention his name back at the clubhouse anymore. All trace of him will be removed from the club's history. Like he was never part of Severed, but that's the rules of the club.

I picture his goofy smile. I can still hear his laugh. It hurts like fuck. I can't count the number of nights me and him stayed up watching his stupid movies. We'd joke around about how many of the moves he'd tried out for real; he even threatened to go get a role in one of them once. I'd love to have seen the club members faces if he'd done that and hit play on the fucker on movie night.

I get now why he wanted Cassie to be closer. I don't know why, call it some sixth sense, but I'm sure she's in danger. If Satan was threatening Disney with his sister then he'll be looking to tie up loose ends. I can't imagine he's in a good mood either. It's clear as shit that Angel was the target today and poor old Disney was just collateral damage. I'm going as fast as I can; weaving in and out of traffic when I come across it, but it's not fast enough. I've got at least an hour on the road yet still.

***

I pull up outside Cassie's apartment. Its dark, no sign of life inside and the porch light is off as well. It's a good neighborhood, mainly small apartments for the college students, but it's normally quiet. There's a party going on at one of the apartments down the end of the street, kids flowing out on to the sidewalk, plastic cups full of god knows what in their hands and loud music thumping through the night air.

I hope to fuck she's there. I move slowly down the path to the front door. My hackles rise as I reach it and see it's ajar. I reach for my piece from the back of my jeans and go on high alert.

I push the door open and my heart falls. It smells like a slaughter house in here. I fumble around on the wall for the light switch. A weak light comes on over my head, fucking energy bulbs. Even though it hasn't warmed up yet there's enough light for me to realize I'm too late. There's fucking blood everywhere. A bloody hand print on the wall slides down towards the carpet, its small enough to be Cassie's. My heart stutters, but I keep walking down the hall, quietly calling out her name. It's like a horror movie has just been shot here.

"Cassie, sweetheart, you there? It's Cowboy, Disney sent me to check on you."

There's no answer.

The kitchen/diner looks pretty normal to me, a few dishes in the sink from breakfast or lunch, but no obvious disturbance so I move past towards the back of the apartment and what I assume is the bedroom.

The bedroom door is thrown wide; when I look it's actually hanging off its hinges. Looks like Cassie put up a fight at least. I step in and see more blood. There's so much of it, and it's covering every surface. I try not to breathe though my nose because the stench of blood is even stronger in this room.

My eyes fall on the bed in the middle of the room. The sheets look like they were a pretty white and silver combination, but not anymore. Now they're a mixture of reds and pinks. Small bloody handprints are smudged everywhere. Two small handprints, right at the top of the sheets, stand out to me. They look evenly spaced and are a dark red. As if the bloodied hands where there for a while, clenching the sheets tight. I dread to think why.

I don't like the images my mind is conjuring up. I can picture what that sick fuck did to her in here. There's no sign of her though as I stand in the doorway so I move further into the room. I cry out as I turn to the alcove that was previously hidden from my view.

Cassie.

She's here, but the sick fuck has nailed her upside down to the wall by her hands and feet like some twisted crucifixion. The bile rises in my throat, but I hold it back.

I collapse onto the end of the bed, holding my head in my hands. I'm too late. I'm too fucking late.

The last thing I could have done for my friend, and I'm too fucking late. Fat tears fall down my face. That's the second time today, but before that, I can't remember the last time I cried. I didn't even cry at my father's funeral. I'm crying for the friend I lost. I'm crying for the little girl I remember throwing up in the air, her blonde hair framing her face so she looked like an angel looking down on me, who now is hanging before me in this morbid pose.

Her body's naked, and there are cuts everywhere. There's even that fucking *S* brand the fucker marks his women with. I can't leave her like this. I need to get her down, cover her up, before I call the emergency services. Shit. Can I call them? This is going to bring a shit storm down on the club. I can't tell them why I came here today because we've hidden Disney's death. I'll call Prez. This is a club decision to make. I just need to get myself together before I make the call.

***

It must have taken a good fifteen minutes before I pulled myself together enough to phone Prez. He's told me to stay put and he'll send a crew to clean it up. We can't report this; there's too much that has gone unreported before this. He's promised me revenge though. Satan is living on borrowed time.

When I look at Cassie, I realize the fucker is losing it. This is the worst I've ever seen him do to anyone. Then again, what he did to Disney was new for him as well. If he's coming apart we've got a better chance at catching him. He's bound to slip up somewhere. I just hope we catch him before anyone else loses their life.

I notice he's left the tool box open on the floor, the hammer and nails discarded beside it. I hope Cassie has some pliers in here. I'll need something like that to get these fucking nails out. I spot them inside the box and reach over to start taking the nails out of her hands.

He's hammered these bastard nails in tight. I get a grip of the head of the nail and pull harder. It comes out of the wall suddenly, and at the same time there's an almost inaudible wheeze at the side of me. I step back, startled. I look around expecting the fucker to jump out at me from the shadows but there's nothing there. Then I realize what it must have been and kick myself for not checking when I walked in. There was so much blood, and she was so still.

Carefully, I place my hand on the side of Cassie's neck. Shit. Fuck! There's a pulse there. It's so faint it's almost nonexistent. With a roar I yank out the rest of the nails quickly, supporting her body so it doesn't fall from the wall when I release the last nail.

I carefully take hold of her, cradling her in my arms and moving her to the bed. "I've got you Cassie, you're safe now sweetheart. I'll get help, you just hold on." I'm sobbing as I say the words to her. Why the fuck didn't I check sooner? I've wasted so much time.

Cassie tries to talk, but it's barely a whisper. As her mouth moves it causes small bubbles of blood to escape. I move my ear next to her mouth, trying to catch the words.

"He's going ... Severed... kill Eve." It takes her ages to get the words out and I can barely hear her. She's so fucking weak. I reach for my phone to call the ambulance, but with that last wheeze I've lost her. Fuck. If I'd called for help sooner she might have made it. Why the fuck didn't I check?

I close her eyes, saying a quiet prayer, asking the angels to keep her safe. I'm not a religious man. You can't see the shit I do and believe, but she was a good person. I hope for her sake there is a better place out there for her.

I lay the discarded comforter over her; the guys will be here later to clean the scene. I'm not waiting for them. Picking up my phone to warn Prez that Satan's on his way for Eve I leave the house, shutting the door behind me. I'm not staying here. I've got work to do. I'm going to track that fucker down if it's the last thing I do. I want to be the one who gets to put a fucking bullet through his fucking head. I think there may be a queue of people wanting to do it, but I sure as hell plan on being there when it happens.

I fire up the bike and turn in the direction of Severed, the guilt that I let her down, that I wasn't quick enough lying heavy in my gut. I break speed limits on the way back, my anger boiling over. I've got a fucking death warrant to serve.

Chapter Twenty Seven

Elle

Considering the fact that I didn't think I had a lot of stuff, I've spent nearly all day packing boxes. Shit, I have way too many clothes, half of them I'd forgotten I had as they've been packed away in boxes under the bed. Many of them still have the store labels on them. They're my guilty pleasure when I'm away travelling and writing. I love to wander round little boutiques and treat myself to gorgeous outfits. Thing is I never wear them. When I travel I tend to wear more sensible, comfortable clothes like jeans and t-shirts. When I'm at home here in Australia I live in shorts and vests.

I finger the soft silk of the blouse I'm packing into the charity bag. It's beautiful, but it's not something that will fit with my new life. I told Ink I wasn't giving up my job, but it's not suitable for work or the clubhouse. It's more suited to someone working a nine to five job in an office. That never was going to be me. I read something once that said women only ever wear a third of the stuff in their wardrobe. That's probably right. I have hangers full of clothes that are 'too good' to wear every day, and yet I never make the effort to go anywhere to wear them.

I'll leave some clothes here. I'm actually keeping the place. It's not that I don't think the future will work out with Ink, but I'm a cautious girl after all. I need somewhere to run back to if it does fail, and if it doesn't, it can be our escape. It's only an hour away from the clubhouse so he can get back if he needs to, but it's far enough away that he won't think about casually dropping in if we're supposed to be having some alone time.

I reach for the brown tape to seal the box of items from my dressing table that I'm taking with me. I don't know where Ink is going to find room for my stuff. His room seems pretty full of his shit as it is, but he assured me that he'll make this work.

I look at the pile of boxes already by the bedroom door and am grateful he's sending a prospect over with the truck. There's too much here to fit in my little car. I'll call the charity tomorrow to come get the bags of stuff I'm leaving outside for them.

I open my underwear drawer to pack it up, fingering the sensible knickers I used to wear with distaste. I bin them. I'll go to the mall tomorrow and treat myself to some more lace for Ink, he'll love that. I get hot just thinking about the look he gets in his eyes when he sees me in the sexy lingerie I wear when he's around. I'm hoping he didn't throw away the stuff I bought in England that I left behind when I walked out.

I wouldn't say it's making me sentimental packing my things up, but it's bringing back memories. The next drawer down contains my scrapbook. It's a history of the writing that I've had published, or the one's I'm proud of anyway. I'm a writer. When times were hard I had to take on jobs I wouldn't have done otherwise. I've written crap just to make a living. I'm lucky that now I get to pick and choose who I write for, I get to choose which articles I want to do. One day my dream is to write a book, but for now that's a distant dream. Maybe by living with Ink at the clubhouse, that dream will happen sooner rather than later. It's not like I won't be surrounded with inspiration around those guys, that's for sure.

I sit down on the bed and look around the room. What's sad is that all of these memories of mine are recent. I've kept nothing from my time in care.

They weren't memories I wanted. I'm proud of how my life has turned out. I've worked hard to have nice things; I have a house I like, clothes I love. But still, I've never called it a home. I'm hoping that I'll find that with Ink. Growing up all I ever wanted was to be loved, have a home and family. I'd given up on that dream, but now Ink's given me hope it might happen. I smile, hugging my scrapbook closer to my chest.

I'm about to go grab a coffee when I hear a truck pull up outside. That's odd. I was sure the prospect was going to arrive in the morning. I reach for my phone and see a missed call from Ink, I must have had it on silent and not realized. I can be ditzy like that at times. Putting the phone down I head for the door to greet the prospect, Ink was obviously ringing to tell me he was coming early. I'm excited. I've only got a few things left to pack, so I can surprise Ink and be back there tonight with him. I can't wait to see the look on his face.

***

Ink

Shit.

Elle's not answering her fucking phone. I need her back here now. I've just heard from Cowboy and it's scaring the shit out of me. Satan's killed Disney's little sister and he's coming after Eve.

I reassure myself that Elle isn't even on the sick fucker's radar, but I'll still be happier when she's back here at the clubhouse with me. She'll kick up a stink when I ask her to stay put. She hates me being all macho and shit on her, but she'll understand it's for her own safety.

I'm still trying to get my head around what else has happened today. Everything was great this morning. I went off to work after a hot morning session with Elle, happy that she'd agreed to move in with me and see where this thing between us is going. And then I get back to the clubhouse to find all hell's let loose.

I can't believe Disney would be a rat. Surely I'd have known, the club would have known? The guy didn't have a sneaky bone in his body, and looking back over the past few weeks, I can't think of anything that would have pointed to him either. He was quieter than normal sure, but he often had times like that. He was either in your face happy all the time or he'd go quiet for a few weeks then come bouncing back.

I grab my keys, shouting to the guys in the bar that I'll be back in a couple of hours. I'm going to go get Elle and bring her back here, I haven't got time for her to check her messages, and if she does, I'll pass her on the road anyway.

***

Eve

Angel is in Prez's office. They're trying to work out what to do next. He's told me some of what's happened today but I'm sure he's holding back. The mood around here is so somber I'm hiding out in our room with Elizabeth. Even she's picked up that something's not right. Everyone's been very tight lipped around her, but she's commented that everyone seems sad today. She wanted to draw them a picture to cheer them up but fell asleep over her crayons.

I move over to her cot and check on her, she's fast asleep still, sucking her thumb. She's got her cuddly koala tightly gripped in her other arm. It's rarely left her side since Angel gave her it back in England.

I hear a text message come through on my phone and smile when I see it's from Elle. The smile soon leaves my face when I read it and see the picture attached.

Elle is slumped on the floor, chained to a wall, a gag covering her mouth. Her eyes are wide, tears shine on her cheeks. I read the message below the picture.

You have a choice to make. Turn yourself over to me or I deliver what's going to be left of Elle to the clubhouse gates. I know she's your friend. I've been watching you and her for days. You've got one hour to get here or I start to cut her up into tiny pieces. Tick Tock

My legs give way, and I fall into a sitting position on the bed. There's an address for the warehouse he's asking me to go to.

I look at my sleeping baby girl, trying to decide what to do. This shit isn't ever going to end; at least, not until he has me. He's proven he's invincible time and again. How many more people are going to have to die because of me? If I don't go then it could be Elizabeth or Angel next. I can't live with that.

I can't believe I'm even considering this. How can I give up a chance of happiness with Angel and Elizabeth? The selfish part of me is shouting at me to stay. But Elle is my friend. I can't sit back and let her die, especially not in my place.

Oh, shit. What do I do? I can't even talk it through with anyone. There's not one person here who would let me go. Not even Ink. I suspect he loves Elle, but even he wouldn't let me swap places with her right now. No, this is a decision that only I can make. I look up the location on my phone and see it will take me nearly an hour to get there. I don't have time to think about this. I have to decide now, one way or the other.

I kiss my sleeping child on her forehead. "I love you all the way to the moon and back and lots, lots more baby girl." I hold back a sob. "Tell Daddy I love him."

I take one last look at my daughter before striding from the room, wondering how in hell I'm going to get out of this place unseen. I know she'll be well loved and looked after here.

I set about trying to find a way out. It's locked down like a fucking fortress today. There has to be a way. If I don't get there soon, Elle will be dead.

Chapter Twenty Eight

Eve

I fall lucky when I sneak outside the clubhouse via the kitchen door. It's laundry day and the van is loading up. Sue is chatting to the delivery driver so I take the opportunity to sneak inside the rear of the van and hide between the oversized laundry bags. The smell inside the van is a mixture of sweaty socks and the delicate perfume of freshly laundered sheets. Sadly, the heat inside the van seems to be letting the sweaty socks win.

I wait until the doors are shut and the van is moving before I pick up my phone, opening the photo app. I scroll through until I find the photo of me, Gabe and Elizabeth laughing in the play area at the clubhouse. We look like a happy family and that's how I want to remember them.

A tear falls down my face as I stare at the image in front of me. Whatever lies ahead for me is going to be tough, it's going to hurt and the sad brutal truth is that I won't be coming back. I'm not stupid; I know what I'm walking into. At least my baby girl has Gabe now. I try to stamp the image in my brain. This is the last thing I want to see before my life ends. I need this memory to stay with me and get me through the ordeal that's coming. I take a last look at the picture, kissing the screen before I shut it.

"I'm sorry." I whisper. "I'll love you both forever."

I scare the crap out of the driver when I bang on the partition between us, when I think we're a safe enough distance away from the club. My mind is losing it already because I think to myself, it could have been worse, he could have been driving a hearse. I snicker to myself.

The driver apologizes profusely for not realizing he'd shut me in. I reassure him it was my fault; I'd been too slow and needed to add something to one of the laundry bags. Thankfully he believes me. He drops me off on the next corner after I refuse his offer of a lift back to the clubhouse. I tell him I'll be fine. There's still enough daylight left for me to enjoy a stroll back there. I wave goodbye, and as the van turns the corner out of sight, I pull up the maps app on my phone.

The warehouse is around forty minutes away by car; luckily we're already on the outskirts of Severed town so I head to where I know the taxi office is located. I check my pocket, ensuring I haven't lost the cash I stashed there earlier. The crinkle of the notes reassures me.

Getting into the cab I give the driver the address and sit back. I open my phone once again, taking a long last look at the family I'm leaving behind.

***

Ink

My hackles rise as I approach Elle's house. Everything is still, too still. Even the birds in the trees are silent. It's fucking freaking me out.

Her car is parked out front, the bonnet warm from the sun, but not from recently being driven. There's no sound from the house which is unusual for Elle. She hates silence. She's always playing music in the background and tunelessly singing along, but I can't hear anything right now. It's deadly silent and I don't like it.

I move towards the front door, my gun ready in my hand. There's no answer to my knock, so I ease the front door open, moving in quietly and stealthily. The table in the hallway is knocked over, lying on its side. My gun rises in reaction to the sight of some sort of struggle. I move on silent feet as I search the house room by room but there's no sign of Elle. I go back through the house a second time, looking for clues. Her purse is still here, along with her wallet and car keys; another sign there's something not right. Elle always has her purse with her. There's no sign of her here and oddly enough no sign of her phone.

An icy chill goes through me. There has to be a simple explanation for her absence, but right now I can't think of one. I take out my phone and dial Angel.

***

Gabe

Can today get any worse?

I've just had Ink on the phone. Elle's missing. The way her stuff has been left at the house and the fallen table lead us both to believe it's Satan's work. I breathe a shaky sigh of relief that it's not Eve. I've got her locked down here and for a good fucking reason. It's the only way I can keep her safe. None of us ever thought Elle would be at risk, she's a stranger as far as Satan is concerned. But then, none of us thought Disney would be the rat either.

I head to my room to go give Eve the news and to ask her if she's heard from Elle today, hoping that there's some simple explanation for her disappearance. Ink's already heading back here in case she knows anything.

Quietly stepping into the room because I know Elizabeth will be asleep I look around for Eve. She's not here. I take a quick look in the bathroom, but come up empty. Elizabeth innocently snores away in her cot. She can't be far; it's not like her to leave her daughter alone, even if she's asleep. She must have popped out for a few minutes. She could be out in the bar or in the back yard so I go in search of her.

By the time I reach the back of the clubhouse I'm getting scared. None of the members I've asked have seen her since she went to put Elizabeth down for her nap. Teresa is over in the corner, laughing with Justice. When she sees the look on my face she stops mid laugh, standing quickly, on high alert.

"What's wrong, Angel?"

"Nothing Tess, just trying to find that woman of mine." I laugh but it even sounds false to me. "She must be playing hide and seek with me and just forgot to tell me."

Teresa frowns, trying to recall when she last saw Eve. "I don't think I've seen her for a few hours. Its Elizabeth's nap time isn't it? I thought she was in your room."

Both Teresa and Justice offer to help me search for Eve, but I assure them I've looked everywhere.
"Where's her phone?" Justice asks. I look at him, puzzled by the question.

"Why?"

"We were comparing apps the other day and I showed her one I have on my phone to help find it if I lose it. I'm sure she said she was going to download it." He pauses. "If she did then we can use it to find her. I just need her phone number."

He leads us into the clubhouse and to his room where he has his laptop set up. He clicks a few buttons then looks to me for the number. He types it in and the screen shows a large map, slowly zooming in closer every few moments.

I groan when I realize the area it's closing in on isn't the clubhouse, it's somewhere further away. The dot keeps stopping then moving. Justice clicks some more buttons and opens up a Google earth image. It's somewhere on the far side of Severed. It's moving away from us all the time.

It can't be. There's no way Eve could have left the clubhouse, and she's on lockdown for fucks sake! I call the gate and shout at Ice to get his arse in here now. He's one of the guards on gate duty this afternoon.

I ask Teresa if she has Elle's phone number and she shakes her head. "She can't be on her way to Elle's though," she says. "Elle lives in the other direction."

Justice is looking at his phone and starts clicking numbers on the first screen again. This time when the screen zooms in it's on a static dot. A static dot in the same direction Eve is heading. What the fuck?
A few more clicks, and the Google earth image changes to show us the new location. It's an old warehouse.

Shit.

My heart falls as I think my worst nightmare is about to come true. There's no good reason for Elle to be in an abandoned warehouse that Eve is heading right towards. There's only one explanation – Satan. I roar out, smashing the lamp from the desk in front of me. Teresa flinches. I look at them both, it's obvious they haven't quite worked it out yet, then Justice swears loudly as he realizes what he's looking at.

"Oh shit, no!"

Teresa pales visibly. "Wh...What's going on?" She stammers.

Justice explains to her what the screen is telling us. While he does that I get Ink on the phone and give him the address Justice has written down, arranging to meet him there. I hang up and dial Cowboy and relay the same message to him before hanging up.

Ice hurries into the room, we go through the visitors this afternoon but I'm none the wiser.

"The laundry truck." Teresa's voice is so quiet, I almost don't hear her. I look at her, my confusion obvious on my face. "It's the only vehicle she could have snuck out in. The timing is right as well."

Shit. It's really happening. For some reason Eve left the safety of the clubhouse. It's got to be connected to Elle.

I ask Justice to keep monitoring both phones and to keep me updated, then ask Teresa to go fill in Prez and ask him to get a team out there to the warehouse as soon so he can. I can't wait any longer, I've got to get out there now and find my woman.

Ice doesn't know what's going on but immediately states that he's coming with me. He lets me know that if it's anything to do with Eve he will do all he can. I thank my brother and we both head out to our bikes. Ice shouting at a few of the other guys to join us as we pass through the clubhouse. Prez will sort out the rest. I can't wait for them though, I need to go now. I pause at the gun room on the way out, grabbing a couple of extras.

Hold on baby, I pray. This shit ends tonight.

If Satan's there, he's a dead man. Only one of us is going to come out of that warehouse alive.

Chapter Twenty Nine

Eve

The taxi drops me off at the end of the lane. He didn't want me walking down here on my own but I assured him I'd be fine before he drove away.

I snicker to myself. *Fine*?

The last thing I am going to be tonight is fine. Pulling myself straighter I move down the lane. He obviously heard the car as he's leaning nonchalantly against the open door, the light from the room behind framing his silhouette. The closer I get, the more his resemblance to Gabe hits me.

How can life be so cruel? It's given me the man of my dreams, and yet that face will be the last one I see as my life drains away. I silently beg a god I've never believed in for help. If he can't save me, and I doubt right now that anything, including God could, then I ask that it happen quickly.

The closer I get to the doorway, the more my steps falter.

When I'm almost within his reach, I see the shit eating grin Satan is wearing. I also notice that even though he and Gabe are identical, they're very different too. Gabe doesn't have the evil look about his face or the permanent scowl ruining his features. Satan oozes evil. Gabe is a dangerous man when it comes to those he loves, but Satan doesn't care for anyone.

Satan's clothing is covered in blood, as if he's taken a shower in the stuff. Fuck, there's so much of it. It's spattered over his face and clothes. Please don't let it be Elle's.

He grabs me roughly by my arm, yanking me toward him. His fetid breath warm against my cheek. I cry out as he licks the side of my face. The sick fuck is lapping away at my tears and by the sounds of his growl he's fucking enjoying it. I try to force myself to stop crying. I don't want to give him the satisfaction.

He drags me into the dimly lit room. My eyes dart around frantically, searching for Elle. There's a body slumped on the floor over by one wall, but it looks lifeless. *No!* I can't have sacrificed my life for hers in vain. He's leading me over to where Elle lays. I see the chain. It's thick, and the shackle on her wrist looks solid. No matter how much she struggles she won't be able to get free. Her wrist looks small inside the shackle, but it's bloodied and raw from where she's fought against it. Her clothing is torn in places and dirty, but looks to be intact, her jeans still fastened. My eyes are taking it all in as Satan grabs another chain and shackle, securing me to the wall next to her. She's not moved in the time it's taken us to walk over here and chain me up. *What have I done?*

It becomes clear to me that even if Elle is still alive, and I hope to god she is, that she won't be released. Both of us are going to die in this dark and dirty place.

Satan laughs hysterically as he looks at me. Oh god, I think he's lost it. He was dangerous before, but now he's a madman. He moves back, admiring his new toy. That's all I am to this monster, a shiny new toy to play with then destroy. I shouldn't have come. I should have known he'd destroy Elle regardless of whether or not I showed up.

"Well, it's about fucking time, Eve. You've led me a merry chase I have to say. It's going to be so sweet killing you." He pulls his phone from his pocket. "I was going to have my fun with you then send your corpse back to lover boy, but it's going to be so much more fun to get him here and let him watch while I fuck you every which way. I'm just dying to cut up that pretty cunt of yours".

He laughs hysterically again. There's a flash as the camera on his phone captures an image, then he taps away on his screen.

I realize I've really fucked up. Coming here was supposed to keep Gabe safe, it was supposed to free Elle. I'm the world's biggest fool. Me coming here has put everyone in danger. How could I have been so fucking stupid?

"Make yourself comfortable Eve; it will take my dear brother at least an hour to get here." He snickers loudly. "If he bothers to check his phone that is. Poor Beth held on for him you know. She was so strong; she put up a real fight." He's smiling at whatever sick memory he's replaying. "Then she realized he wasn't coming to save her and she lost all her fight. So disappointing." He looks back to me, a greedy expression on his face. "You'll fight me though, won't you Eve?" He smiles.

If I fight, then this sick fuck wins. As much as I want to, I can't fight back; I won't give him that satisfaction. He will revel in my pain and struggle; I have to take what he gives me and not show too much emotion. The more I give him, the more pleasure he gets out of all this. But he's sent for Gabe. As much as my death will destroy him, I can't let him watch it. I have to do something now. Somehow, I have to taunt him into killing me before Gabe gets here. I rack my brain for anything I can use against him. I have no weapons, I'm chained to this wall for fuck sake, and the only tool I have left is words. I need to use them cleverly if this is going to work. But how?

Elle moans, stirring at the side of me. Thank god she's alive. She lifts her battered face to mine, a silent no forming on her lips. She looks defeated. Satan smirks even more when he sees her expression.

"I'll leave you girls to say goodbye to each other." He laughs again. "You've got a few minutes while I go get some more of my tools. Make the most of them." Just before he leaves the room he turns back to us. "Don't worry, you'll have plenty of time to catch up properly later. You'll be together for eternity when you meet back up in hell." He's laughing hysterically as he leaves the room.

***

Gabe

We cut the engines on the bikes; we can't afford to let him know we're almost there. Cowboy and Ink both joined us on route. With me, Ice, and the guys we brought along, there are ten of us. I pull out my phone to see if there's any news from Justice or Prez and see there's a new message from an unknown number. I can't go through this again. Cowboy sees my hesitation, when he sees what's on the phone screen he snatches it from my hand, opening the message himself as he quickly walks away from me.

"Fuck!" The word escapes his mouth before he can stop it. Ink groans beside him. Whatever they've seen isn't good.

"Tell me." I growl.

Cowboy passes me the phone back instead, shaking his head. It's a picture of Eve; she's chained up like a fucking animal. There's someone slumped at the side of her, I'm guessing that's Elle. The message tells me I've got an hour to get here and watch my girl die. If I don't get here in time he'll draw her death out so it's even more painful than if I was watching. I want to crush the phone in my grasp. That fucker is a dead man. He's dying tonight; I'll make fucking sure of it.

Ink is on the phone to someone, checking where our back up is I guess. I look back at my phone and something strikes me. He's given me an hour. He doesn't think I know where Eve is until now. That's an hour he's going to regret giving me, and I'm going to use it wisely.

I call the guys together, laying out my plan. My last instruction is clear. They can hurt Satan, but they can't kill him. I want to be the one to put a bullet between that fucker's eyes. Cowboy and Ink look pissed, but they agree. We've got about fifteen minutes before Prez and the guys arrive so we set off down the lane, quietly and stealthily. We need to check out the building, find the best way in, and the best way out for the girls.

I grip my gun tightly. Tonight I'm going to set Eve free from the nightmare she's been living since I met her. I'm going to take my girl home and never let her go. First though, I've got the fucking devil to kill. Bring it on.

***

Eve

Elle's barely responsive. I'm worried about her. There's a bad gash on her head. I think she may have a concussion; she's sure as shit in shock as well. I reach for her hand, patting it and murmuring quiet words of encouragement. I tell her we'll be fine, our men will find us. I hope she can't hear the lie in my voice. Our men can't find us because I was a stupid cow who didn't think it through. I rushed into a decision I shouldn't have made, and it's going to get us both killed. I should have gone straight to Gabe. He'd have known how to save Elle. But no, I didn't fucking think.

Elle doesn't respond. Her eyes stare off into the distance, watching the door Satan left through. I know when he's back because she stiffens; wincing at the pain the movement causes her.

He's whistling. The fucker is whistling a Disney song. "Whistle while you work."

He places a tool pouch on a table, pulling the table closer to us. I spot the glint of metal, the reflection from the weak light bulb overhead sparkling off the sharp edges of a pouch full of knives. I grit my teeth. I've seen what Satan can do with a knife before. I've heard how he brands his women. I've also heard what he does when he's had enough. I shudder at the thought of a sharp, cruel blade being inserted there, of the unimaginable pain, of enduring that pain as your life's blood slowly seeps out of you.

I turn to Elle, she's not watching him. She's gone back into that safe place inside her head I guess. I wish I could go there, but it's not happening for me. I'm transfixed instead by the glint of the blades. Satan is taking them out one at a time, sharpening them, cradling them like babies for fucks sake. I start to shake. I can't help myself. I find myself wishing he'd just ended it with a bullet that day back in the store. So many people have died because he didn't. Their blood is on my hands. The tears I've held at bay start to fall slowly down my face.

Elle's eyes move slowly towards the door. Has she seen something? I know time has passed slowly, but there's no way it's been an hour. The MC is almost an hour away, even if Gabe read the text message straight away it's too soon for him to be here. I dismiss it as something she's imagining instead, especially when her eyes light up. There's only one thing that puts that light in her eyes and Ink's not going to be coming here.

There's a rustling noise, I can't quite identify it, or the direction it came from. Satan must have heard it as he looks round the room, his head turning in all directions before coming over and grabbing Elle. He holds the gun between her eyes.

"Come out you fuckers, I know you're there. Move slowly to the center of the room and put your guns down on the floor. Kick them over to me." He's gone mad. There's no one there. He clicks back the safety catch on the gun. That's when I see them. For a moment I think I'm hallucinating, like Elle.

From each of the other corners of the room they appear, Ink, Cowboy, and my Angel. Now I know I'm hallucinating. Their hands are held high, their guns on show. They advance towards us.

"Put the fucking guns down now!" Satan screams. I watch in disbelief as the guys lower their guns to the floor, before backing away again slowly, hands back in the air.

I let out the breath I've been holding. Don't they realize they can't trust this crazy fucker? He turns away from me a little and I take my chance. If the guys won't save me, I will.

I leap to my feet, wrapping the long chain I'm fastened to around his neck and pulling tight. He drops the gun he was holding, turning quickly, he smashes his fist in my face. Shit! He broke my nose. It all happens so quickly. One hand reaches for the back of his jeans and then the next second, there's a gun pointing at me, at my head.

"You crazy bitch!" He screams. "You're fucking dead."

There's a loud bang, a woman's scream and the thump of a body hitting the floor. My ears are ringing from the gunshot, it was so close. I can't see Angel. I scream for him, but my mind can't handle the stress anymore and I black out.

Epilogue

One month later

???

There's no conversation in the room, just the steady buzz of the tattoo gun. The CD player is quietly playing one of my favorite songs by Imagine Dragons 'Demons'.

I'm getting the tattoo on my hip. I thought long and hard about what I wanted; there's a reason behind every element of this tattoo.

The words surrounding it is one of my favorite quotes; it represents the huge changes that have occurred in my life these last couple of months. I never thought my life would change so drastically.

The tattoo gun stops. It's done. I suck a deep breath in, inhaling that peculiar smell that's only found in tattoo shops. It's like burned ink, but it's a sweet smell, one I've grown to love.

I look at the sketch of my tattoo I've been clutching in my hands. In the center there's a skull. That represents death, more specifically my role in a man's death. We all pulled the trigger at the same time so I guess we'll never know which bullet was responsible. All that matters is a man died because of me, and I need to remember that. The words above and below the skull represent my life, before and after his death.

Every Saint has a past, every sinner has a future.

Killing a man is a sin. I have to live with that knowledge. But even a sinner like me deserves a chance, and that's where the future comes in.

Woven in and out of the skull are roses. They represent my strength. Beautiful to look at, but watch out for that thorn, it bites. I may be beautiful, but I've got an inner strength I've kept hidden. No more. I'm not afraid to show my strength anymore.

Ink

I put the tattoo gun down on the table, and then wipe the tattoo over with my cloth. It's red and angry but looks great against her pale skin. I'm so fucking proud of Elle. I thought I'd lost her that night in the warehouse. I almost lost it when that crazy fucker held his gun against her head. Eve surprised us all by trying to strangle him with that chain. He surprised us even more when he pulled the second gun.

Angel screamed when Satan turned the gun on Eve. The stupid fucker always carried a backup gun, but he should have known we would too. I think we all drew at the same time. It sounded like one very loud shot, but in reality there were four of us. We all shot him, but only one of us hit the sick fuck between the eyes, the killing shot.

When he turned the gun on Eve it triggered something in Elle. She reached down, grabbed the gun he'd dropped and pulled the trigger at the same time as the rest of us.

She has nightmares about it most nights. She can't make peace with her part in it. I know Cowboy, Angel and I haven't lost any sleep over it though. Crazy fucker needed to die. He'd destroyed too many lives.

Eve is still looking over her shoulder. By the time she came round, the backup team had arrived and we'd cleaned up the scene. She never saw his body so she won't believe he's dead. She's constantly on alert, expecting him to pop up whenever she goes out.

Angel has a surprise for her today; we're all hoping it helps.

I pull my woman closer to me, holding her tight, yet careful to avoid the tender area where I've just inked her. She's refused to come to my room at the shop until today. She knows this is where I fucked Emma. I'm hoping I've healed that, given her different memories of this room to take away. We made love in here before her tattoo. On the table. Against the wall. Straddling my chair. I know now I love her. Deep down I love her. But it's too soon to tell her that yet. I'll give it a little longer, but before the year's out she'll be my old lady.

Claimed and official.

***

Gabe

I take a deep breath and hunt down Eve. I'm pretty sure she'll be in our room as she told me she was going to give Elizabeth a bath.
I open the door and I'm greeted by loud giggling and squealing. I look to the bed. Eve's bent over a wriggling Elizabeth. She's blowing raspberries on Elizabeth's chubby belly.

"Mummy!" Elizabeth squeals.

A smile creeps on my face and I pounce on Eve. I tackle her to the bed, lifting her top to reveal her stomach.

"Gabe, what are you-" I cut her off, blowing a raspberry on her belly, just like she did with Elizabeth and she giggles.

Elizabeth laughs loudly and begins bouncing on the bed. "Get mummy!"

After our little play, Eve finally gets Elizabeth dressed and ready. I decide it's time.

With sweaty hands and a fast beating heart I look at my beautiful lady. "Eve, I need to show you something."

I see in her eyes that there's a little panic. After all the shit Satan put her through she still doesn't truly believe it's all over.

"What?" She asks, picking up Elizabeth.

"It's good I promise." I smile at her.

***

I bring my black SUV to a stop, and I begin to sweat.

Fuck I've never been this nervous in my life!
I've brought down men, dealt with frightening and life threatening situations and nearly lost Eve to *him*, but I swear, I've never been this fucking nervous. Truthfully, I'm fucking scared too.

I take a risk and glance at Eve who is sitting in the passenger seat. Her eyes are bright and staring, confused at what she's seeing in front of her.

She looks to me. "Gabe?"

I open my door and quickly walk around to her side. Elizabeth, who is sitting in her booster seat, is too busy playing with her dolls to care about us at the minute. I hold Eve's hand as she slowly gets out of the car. Her eyes widen at the sight in front of us.

I turn her towards me so we're standing chest to chest, my arms wrapped around her back.

Eve

I gaze into his dark, beautiful blue eyes as he looks down at me. "Eve, I told you that when you were completely safe that I would get our family a home." I'm stunned as he turns me around to face the beautiful building in front of me.

I look at the house; it looks a little larger than an average house, but not too big. Pretty windows are scattered amidst the cream colored brick work. A lush green garden spreads out in front, a large private fence protecting the back. Surrounding the front garden there's a little white picket fence that almost makes me laugh.

I feel Gabe lean down to my ear. "That time is now, baby. Welcome home."

Happy tears fall, I can't believe it. I'm finally safe. Gabe wouldn't get me the house we wanted if we were still in danger. The tension and fear I've been feeling falls away. I'm left an emotional wreck as I watch Gabe get an excited Elizabeth out of the car. He laughs as she plants a wet, sloppy kiss on his cheek.

Once Gabe puts Elizabeth down she goes straight for the white wooden gate, running in circles around the front garden. This is it. This is the life I've always wanted for myself and my baby girl.

Gabe holds my hand, guiding me inside our new home. I take a deep breath, letting it all sink in. I watch Gabe and Elizabeth explore and happily follow them.

I'm where I'm meant to be.

I'm home.

THE END

Acknowledgements

There is no way we could have created this book without our fantastic team of beta readers. We owe a huge debt of gratitude to Elle, Emma, Ellen, Nessa, Vickie, Angi and Jane. There were times when we left them hanging in suspense, and we had them shouting and swearing at us for some of the plot twists they hadn't been expecting. Their input was invaluable. Their reactions were priceless. Thank you from the bottom of our hearts.

Thank you to the readers who bought Severed Angel (Severed MC #1), your feedback and responses have been amazing and we are truly humbled and honored by your sharing them with us. We just hope that this second book lives up to your expectations.

Thank you to the bloggers who have supported us all the way through this crazy journey. To Kelly of Kelly's Kindle Konfessions who introduced K.T Fisher and Ava Manello to each other, without you there'd never have been a book one. To Charlie & Mel's book reviews who have shared nearly every single one of our teasers and been in constant contact awaiting book two, and to everyone who shared a cover reveal, teaser or hosted an author takeover, thank you.

To the authors we love and who we admire, thank you for writing such great books. You inspire us daily. And to those authors who have supported us in this journey, words cannot express our thanks enough.

And yes... we're fangirls and in absolute shock still that you took time out to do that for us. We love you.

About K.T Fisher

I love reading, it's my favourite hobby. I've always had ideas for my own books packed into my head so I thought I would write them out for people to enjoy

Stalk K.T. Fisher

Facebook:
https://www.facebook.com/pages/KTFisher/490003474414733?ref=ts&fref=ts

Twitter: @KTFisher_Author

Goodreads: https://www.goodreads.com/KTFisher

About Ava Manello

I'm a passionate reader, blogger, publisher, and author. I love nothing more than helping other Indie authors publish their books - be that reviewing, beta reading, formatting or proofreading, I love erotic suspense that's well written and engages the reader, and I love promoting the heck out of it over on my book blog http://www.kinkybookklub.co.uk

Stalk Ava Manello

Facebook: http://www.facebook.com/avamanello

Twitter: @AvaManello

Goodreads: https://www.goodreads.com/AvaManello

Website: http://www.avamanello.co.uk

Made in the USA
Charleston, SC
09 June 2014